2-6 Mafia: Murder on the Horizon

By:
Selo Sunkist

Cadmus Publishing
www.cadmuspublishing.com

DEDICATION

This book is dedicated to my family and loved ones I have met along life's journey. Mountains have been moved. I give a special thanks to Jalyse McDougald for giving birth to our beautiful daughter Zionna. Daddy loves you and everything I do is for you. Thanks to Cadmus Publishing for being a part of my dreams and for bringing a dream to a reality.

Selo Sunkist is:
CEO of Zionna International Organization
Negotiating National Assistance LLC
And Zionna's Fashion Boutique
Author
Community Activist
Entrepreneur
Philanthropist
Poet

Table of Contents

CHAPTER 1

The chief of the Fayetteville Police Department sat patiently at his desk waiting on Ms. Martinez to enter his office. William Grey was in his late forties and held the title as the youngest police chief in Cumberland County. For the last two years Grey made the streets of Fayetteville manageable for citizens to perform their daily tasks. Grey eliminated the fear of being robbed as you are pumping your gas at the local gas station or just going on a morning run.

William Grey was from the streets of New York and knew the hood like the back of his hand. He had seen it all and now that he sits in an influential and prestigious seat, he planned to run it all. Looking at his exclusive Omega Moonwatch he saw that it was going on 10 o'clock. He exhaled with frustration. Time is money and God knows you can't get an hour back.

His office door opened, and his secretary stood in the doorway with an unpleasant expression. She was getting ready to speak when Grey's phone rang. She shot him a look wishing he would pick that phone up. Noticing her demeanor, he declined the phone call. Ms. Alexus White had been his secretary for the last year and he knew when she was pissed. "How may I help you, Ms. White?"

"For starters you can say good morning, and for seconds your daughter has been blowing up the office phone for the last hour trying to reach you. Your 10 o'clock is here as well. Should I send her in?"

"Yeah, you can send her in," Grey replied. Grey cleared his desk. Cleanliness is next to godliness, he thought. Seconds later he heard a knock on the door.

"You can come in." Grey sat back in his chair and waited for Ms. Alisha Martinez to enter.

"Sorry I was late but 401 was backed up this morning," Martinez said while holding her hand out to greet the chief of police.

Grey stood and accepted her hand. "Nice to meet you. You may have a seat."

Martinez sat and adjusted herself to meet her comfort. Once she was settled, she reached in her purse to retrieve a letter of recommendation given to her by her aunt and Cumberland County district attorney Amanda Koontz. She handed the letter to Grey. What was Amanda up to this time, Grey thought as he accepted the letter.

> *Dear Mr. Grey,*
> *Keep her safe and under your wing. I owe you one.*

He closed the letter and placed it in his pocket.

"I see you know people in high places," Grey said as he opened his laptop and waited for her to reply.

"I guess you can say that," adding more of her Hispanic accent than was needed.

Alisha Martinez was the definition of exquisite. She was black and Hispanic. Standing at five-foot-seven she had a body to die for. She was light skinned in complexion, skin the color of Beyonce. She weighed 165 pounds and would put you in the mind of a young Priyanka Jonas. Her jet-black hair was waist length. She had emerald-green eyes that matched her mother's.

Grey cleared his throat and dropped his stare. "You will be working directly under me and will take orders from me. I have formed an undercover unit called Operation Black Ops. You will be working as an undercover intelligence officer. The unit is very hands-on and is in the street heavily. You will have to be fast on your feet and be a quick thinker. Our field officer is Stacy Fisher. He will train you. You will learn how to maneuver in dangerous situations. I'm looking at your file and I see you have taken Social Interaction. You will be dealing with all walks of life who will take your life without a second thought. You will need those skills. Officer Stanburg is the captain over this unit. He will be in touch. You will start your training in 24 hours, so get a good night's rest."

"Ms. Martinez, you came recommended so I expect nothing but greatness from you." Grey stood, reaching in his desk to retrieve a golden shield. "Here! Wear it with pride," Grey said while passing Martinez her badge.

Her eyes lit up with joy knowing all of her hard work had finally paid off. She was speechless but relished the moment. "Thank you, sir," she said exuberantly. She stood there in perfect peace, lost in her own thoughts.

Grey gave her body a quick look over. He appreciated the true beauty of a woman. He could feel his dick getting hard and knew it was time for Martinez to go. He broke his stare and opened the office door for her to leave.

"Thank you for giving me this opportunity, and I promise I would never underestimate the level of gradation you have shown.

"You are welcome, and don't forget to get a good night's rest. Believe me, you're going to need it."

"I will, Mr. Grey," Martinez acknowledged Ms. White as she exited the office. Grey watched as she left. Damn, she bad.

"Hello? Are you going to call your daughter or are you going to keep your eyes glued on that young girl's ass?" Ms. White said, snapping her fingers in Grey's face.

He shut the office door in her face and returned to work.

CHAPTER 2

"Baby, can we stop and get something to eat? I'm starving."
Trearina had been driving for the last three hours. She was
hungry, sleepy, and had to piss like crazy. Passing the last
exit she saw a couple of food spots, so she tried her luck knowing if it was up to Sunkist, they would keep it pushing until they
reached Fayetteville.

He was focused on getting these 20 bricks back to Fayetteville.
Sunkist looked over at the fuel level. "Yeah, I guess we can make
a pit stop. We got to fill up anyway."

Trearina cut her eyes at Sunkist, knowing if it wasn't for the
chance, they would run out of gas her ass would still be heading
down I-95. Niggas ain't shit, she thought as she pulled into a Shell
gas station.

Sunkist jumped out to pump the gas. "You want anything?"
Trearina asked.

"Nah, I'm good," Sunkist said while turning his attention to
his cell. He checked the time—6:45 p.m. He would be in the Ville

in about 35 more minutes. Everything was looking good. He decided to call Pressure.

Pressure was one of his homies from Durham. They met back in the day on the yard at Craven while they were processing. He'd seen that Pressure was a real dude, so he put him on the team and introduced him to the rest of the criminal family. Pressure's position was to oversee that the bricks got moved correctly with less liability.

Sunkist scrolled down his list of contacts and tapped on Pressure. Pressure picked up on the second ring.

"What's good, big homie? Salute Capital Hz."

"Capital Hz. Look, I'm about 35 minutes from the Ville so be ready when we pull up. Matter of fact, I'm going to have Trearina drop me off at my spot in Hope Mills. I got some shit to handle before this nigga skip town."

"Facts, homie. Shit, you know I got shit covered on my end."

"Fuck! Look, homie, I got to go."

Sunkist ended the call as a state trooper pulled up beside him. The trooper parked and got out. Trearina came out the store talking on her phone. "Bitch, that nigga lame if he still waiting," Trearina said.

"Oh, so you Megan Thee Stallion now," Anna said on the other end of the phone, making fun of her friend Trearina.

"You real funny. At least he not no…" Trearina stopped in her tracks when she saw the state trooper at the gas pump. She caught eye contact with Sunkist. He looked at her then towards the driver's seat. She picked up on the nonverbal communication. Trearina could hear Anna saying something on the other end of the phone. She hit the end button, disconnecting the call. She could hear her heart pounding in her chest. Beads of sweat began formulating on her forehead. She could tell that the cop was watching her. She cursed under her breath "fuck." This wasn't the day to be cute. Trearina put her head down and walked as quickly as she could toward the Chevrolet Equinox. She opened the door and got in. Her heart was still racing.

She looked through the passenger side window, hoping to see if Sunkist was coming. The passenger side mirror was too far out. She was too scared to turn around, so she kept both hands on the wheel and stared forward.

Sunkist placed the pump back on the station. The air seemed to get cooler as the time passed. Sunkist opened the door to the SUV and got inside. "Let's go," he barked. Trearina put the SUV in drive. A knock came from the passenger side window.

Trearina didn't know what to do. She was frozen to her seat. She looked at Sunkist who played it cool. Sunkist let down his window. "May I help you, officer?"

"You may need this," the officer said and held up Sunkist's cellphone. "You left it on top of the gas pump."

"Thank you, sir," Sunkist said as he got his phone from the officer.

"Y'all have a nice night," the officer said as he returned to his vehicle.

Sunkist let up his window and exhaled, finally releasing his finger off the trigger of his XD-40.

Trearina pulled out of the gas station and hopped back on I-95.

Sunkist laid his seat back and closed his eyes, zoned out to the sound of Lil Baby lyrics. As he rode his thoughts reflected the past. Life was short and in this lifestyle life can be snatched from you in the blink of an eye.

Sunkist was born at the Children's Hospital in Philly. His mother at that time was on drugs and embraced the streets like the lines on a highway. His father was a hands-on type of guy from North Carolina. You know, the guy you can call for anything. He can fix your car, repair your roof, and sell drugs.

His father was from a small town called Bunnlevel. A place where everybody knew everybody. You had to be careful dating 'cause the bloodlines run deep and close together. When Sunkist was old enough to fend for himself, he jumped off the porch headfirst and deep into the streets. He found Fayetteville and embraced it as home. Many years later his family relocated to the Ville and started a new chapter in their lives.

"Wake up, Joe." Trearina was one of the few people that could call Sunkist by his government.

"A'ight, look! I need you to take the work to Pressure and drop it off. I got some shit to handle." Sunkist opened the door and got out, closing the door behind him.

Trearina was mad 'cause she thought once they dropped the work off she was gonna get some dick. Now she was shit out of luck. Even though she was mad, her loyalty was forever Sunkist's. He had broken her heart. She had fallen deep in love with him before she even knew it. She told herself she would never let herself go, but some things you just couldn't help.

He was light skinned with honey-brown eyes. He had long dreads and stood approximately five-foot-nine. Yeah, the nigga was fine, but that shit come a dime a dozen. It was the way he walked. The way his swag pulls you in. The way he spoke that made your pussy crave him. The nigga had a key to my house. Had my credit cards and bank account information. My children loved him, and my mother gave her approval. Shit! I didn't even know his real name. More or less, I hadn't even fucked him yet.

She snapped out of her trip down memory lane and pulled off. Sunkist reached in his pocket retrieving the keyless remote to his Alfa Romeo. The car was one of his pride and joys. He had it customized with trap compartments specialized for his guns. The car was black on black and blended perfectly with the night. He hopped in and pulled off.

Chapter 3

That's my best friend. She's a real bad bitch. Got her own money. Fire sang along to one of her favorite songs as she got dressed. Born Unique Spellmen, Fire was one of the baddest bitches in Fayetteville. She was black and Asian, 152 pounds. She stood five-foot-six with thick hips and a small waist. Her honey-brown dreads came to her shoulders which matched her honey-brown eyes. She was the true definition of beauty.

In her 22 years life had built her to manage the worst storms. When you look up the word gangsta you get the definition that defines her. She never knew her father, just heard stories of him by her mother. He was some sort of Army official. With him being in the Army, her mother moved to Fayetteville. She was very close to her mother, so the "26" became her home as well.

The men in this city were a disappointment. The women, on the other hand, were a different story. She had never seen so many bad bitches in one place. She was bisexual but never could be in a relationship with a woman. Females gossip too much for her. She hadn't been with a man since she was 20.

She had married her high school sweetheart and became a housewife. After an ordeal between them that broke their relationship, her pussy wouldn't get wet for a man after her relationship demise. She began questioning her sexuality. She found that she enjoyed the comfort of being in a man's presence, but her pussy dripped for a woman.

She could see a set of car lights pulling into her driveway. She went to the window, slid the curtain aside, and peeked out. She knew that there were only two people that knew where she stayed—her mother and Sunkist. Seeing the Alfa Romeo pulling into her driveway she knew her man was home.

She hurried to get dressed knowing time was valuable, 'specially on this nigga's watch. She went to her closet and retrieved two Glock 40s. She held them up and kissed them—my pride and joy. Since she didn't have kids, she grew to love guns. She took a minute to look around her house before leaving. She cut the lights off and locked her door. She was dressed in all black. Only thing that stood out was the tip of her dreads peeking from under her hoodie.

She got in the car. "What's up, baby daddy?" Fire was being extravagant in her greeting. Sunkist looked at Fire with diversity thinking to himself, she is a creature of impetuousness when it comes to her loyalty. Normally when it was time to handle business all games end, but they knew each other like the back of their hands.

Sunkist chose to stick to the code of the streets, ignoring his wants to be playful. He knew an atrocious situation never come half-stepping 'cause your life can be in the hands of another.

Sunkist spoke with fortitude in his voice letting Fire know playtime was over. "You ready? 'Cause tonight's agenda is murder in the first degree."

Fire pulled back the hammer…click. She checked the pistol to see if one was in the head. She smiled, satisfied at what she saw. "Nigga! You ready?" she spoke with venom. It was simply amazing how she could transform into a beast within seconds.

"Look, I'm not trying to question you on this shit, but who the fuck is Mad-Max?" Fire asked. "I mean, I know the nigga A.p. 'cause I use to get my hair done by his girl, Star."

"A'ight, listen. The nigga A.P. had Mad-Max robbing all the dope boys in the Ville. Well, him and the little nigga Sosa. When they got locked up A.p. flipped and went state, snitching on Mad-Max and Sosa. Word get back up north to Killa Ru, now Killa Ru wants that nigga's head. We got allegiance with them, so it came across my desk from the big homie NappBasher. That's big country, Lil homie, so you know shit is real."

"Say no more, let's handle this," Fire spit.

Sunkist received a text. He checked the message.

Text: the nigga A.p. just pulled up to his mama house over here behind Douglas Bird.

Sunkist quickly texted back: We on our way

Sunkist's sister Helena had been following A.p. all night waiting for the perfect moment when he would be most vulnerable. This was the moment, plus his two shooters was locked up. Helena sat, patiently waiting for her brother to pull up. Earlier that afternoon she had stolen a late model Buick from a Super Walmart parking lot. It was perfect for this type of activity.

Helena could see her brother pulling up. She quickly exited the car as her brother parked on the opposite side of the street. Helena seen two figures exit the car and knew the other person had to be Fire. Helena threw the keys to her brother, spoke, and got the hell out of sight.

Sunkist and Fire got in the stolen Buick. "What the fuck, this shit smell like old gym socks." Fire wrinkled her nose. Sunkist just shook his head at her remarks.

"Yo, the nigga coming out now," Fire shouted, gripping her baby.

"Why the fuck are you shouting for?" Sunkist said, but before he got a response Fire was out of the car.

CHAPTER 4

"Why you always coming to see me so late, Anthony?" A.p.'s mother was standing in the living room waiting on a response from yours truly, her son.

"Mom, It's crazy out here in these streets. I got to lay low for awhile until this court shit is over."

"I didn't raise you like this, Anthony. Don't nothing good happen in them streets. I don't want to say it, but if you stay in them streets you are going to end up back in jail or worse. I don't want to be picking my son's casket out, do you hear me? Trust and believe I'm not coming to get your black ass out of jail."

See, that's why I don't come to see you, he thought. His mother never curses so he knew she was mad. He reached in his pocket and pulled out a roll of money, peeling off $500.

"Here, take this money, it will help out on the bills or you can go play bingo."

She took the money and shut up immediately. "Now, I love you, Anthony, but I'm serious."

He kissed his mother, reassuring her that he would be okay. "I'm about to leave, do you need anything else before I go?" he asked. At that moment A.p.'s little sister came running down the hall with her arms wide open. She was only three years old and loved her big brother to death. A.p. picked her up and placed her on his hip. "What's up, big girl?"

"Me and Star was playing hide and go seek," the little girl said.

Star came out of the bathroom. "Y'all ready to go, I told your mother I would be back in the morning," Star said. Star walked over and gave Ms. Mary a hug and kiss. "I will see you in the morning."

"Can you take me to the store?" the little girl asked, giving her big brother the puppy dog eyes. A.p. laughed. She hugged her brother and refused to let go.

A.p. looked at his watch. It was 11:45 at night. Most of the stores were closed. A.p. thought for a second and remembered the iPad Pro he bought earlier from a booster on the murc. It would be the perfect gift. "I got a surprise for you, but you got to close your eyes." She placed her hands over her eyes.

"Star, we will be right back," A.p. told his girl. Him and his little sister headed out the front door, closing the door behind them. A.p. instantly froze, not out of fear, but out of not being in control of an atrocious situation.

Fire pressed her Glock 40 against his temple. He got caught slippin'. "Put the kid down, nigga," Fire spit, pressing the gun harder against his head.

"What the fuck y'all want? I ain't got shit but a couple grand in my pockets. Take that shit and keep it pushing," A.p. spit. A.p. was contemplating on trying Fire since she was so close to him. The thought quickly vanished when he saw Sunkist step out of the shadows. What the fuck is this nigga doing here, he thought.

"Nigga, I'm going to ask you one more time to put the kid down," Fire said, gritting her teeth. His little sister still had her eyes closed but he could feel her shaking and knew she was scared. A.p. knew the only reason he was still living was because of his little sister and there was no way in hell he was putting her down.

"What I suppose to be, scared or something?" A.p. said, grilling Sunkist. "Nigga, what…." Boom! A.p.'s head opened up like a can of tomato sauce. Fire kept pulling the trigger as A.p.'s body fell to the ground.

The little girl hit the ground. She balled up and started crying. Fire stood over the little girl. "I'm sorry," Fire whispered as she aimed her weapon at the little girl's head.

"Let's go," Sunkist barked, breaking Fire out of her trance. Fire lowered her weapon. They ran back to the car, jumped in, and peeled off.

CHAPTER 5

S tanding in lineup, Helena listened to the brief her captain gave. After they were briefed, Helena was assigned to a housing unit. She looked at her Apple watch—6:20 a.m. God, this was going to be a long day. She made her way to her pod, speaking to a couple of other detention officers. She reached H.B.D. housing unit and waited on the breakfast cart so she could feed the detainees once she was stationed in her pod.

After about five minutes the food cart arrived. She entered H.B.D. and relieved the nightshift officer. She clocked in and checked her equipment. Everything was up and running. She cleared her radio check and began to serve breakfast. She began with the bottom level. Damn, I forgot to make my rounds, she thought.

She quickly grabbed her clock and inmate picture book. Helena Johnson knew most of the offenders because she either knew them from school or knew them from the streets. "What the hell you doing in here, Lil Buck? I just seen your sister yesterday and she told me you was doing good." Lil Buck just hung his head in disappointment. "I'll talk to you later," she said.

She finished her rounds and made breakfast call. She popped the first six cells so the detainees could come get their breakfast. Shaggy Sean was talking and trying to see the numbers on the games last night, so he was taking his time while everyone else rushed to get their food. "Boy! Bring your ass on. I got to get my cell searches done." Shaggy grabbed his breakfast.

"Yo, tell your sister I said what's up," he said with a devilish grin.

"They moved her to transportation and since you want to be a smartass you tell her when you get out of jail," Helena said with much attitude. She used to fuck with Shaggy Sean back in the day when he was his shit.

She finished serving breakfast just in time to make her next clock. She grabbed the visitation list so she could let the ones that were on her list know they had a visit today. She started her rounds. She got to cell 114 and stopped. "Boy, if you don't put that little shit up I'ma mace your nasty ass." She continued to make her rounds.

The other offenders started clowning the dude she just played. She looked at her watch—7:05. Her cell searches would have to wait. It was rec time.

An offender shouted from the upper level, "Rec time."

"I know what time it is. Sit your ass down before I don't let you out." She took her sweet time getting back to the control desk. She thought to herself; God, I'm so petty. She punched in her staff I.D., unlocking the panel. She let out the top level for their one-hour recreational period.

Helena adjusted in her seat and picked up the phone to call her sister, Tasha. Tasha picked up on the second ring. "Hey, big sis."

"Hey, my ass. You know I'm mad at you."

"I know, but I promise you I'm going to make up for missing your birthday."

"Bitch, you better. Where did they reassign you to?"

"They still got me in transportation. Oh yeah, do you know Lil Danny?"

"From the dooms."

"Yeah, that's him. The nigga going to Craven today. After he cuts a bitch head off, I'm the one that got to transport him."

"Be careful. You know, he use to fuck with my nigga L'Skeet and both them niggas crazy. So, how about this nigga Shaggy Sean tried me talking 'bout tell your sister I said what's up."

"He better get a bond. What's up with 40? I heard the feds got him. I know everybody fucked up, plus 30 just died."

"Yeah, 30 was my heart. I started fucking with him when Wanda started dating crimes. The whole darkside camp is falling apart."

"Well, let me go so I can get back to work."

"Okay, I'll talk to you later. Oh, have you heard from Bia?"

"Nah, not lately."

"Never mind, talk to you later, bye!"

CHAPTER 6

etective Andrew McPhereman and Brad Selmon were the first two on the scene. Detective McPhereman parked the police car. "Where the hell is county at?" he questioned. "I guess the real police have to handle real police work."

Selmon thought McPhereman's statement was funny 'cause he used to be a county sheriff before becoming a Fayetteville police detective. He just smiled and kept his comment to himself.

Ms. Mary and Star were standing on the porch waving their hands. They exited the vehicle and made their way up the driveway. "Oh my God, them son of a bitches killed my only son!" Ms. Mary screamed. She tumbled backwards and grabbed her chest. She couldn't breathe.

Star ran to her aid. "Mama, are you okay?" Star couldn't believe her eyes. Ms. Mary wasn't responding. "Somebody call 9-1-1, we need an ambulance!" Star shouted. She looked around for her phone 'cause the police were just standing there. Star ran in the house to call 9-1-1.

Little Malisha, A.p.'s little sister, just sat on the porch with her head down. She just stared at the white sheet their mother placed over his body. She could comprehend the missing element of life and knew her big brother was dead.

After the 9-1-1 call Star returned outside. Detective McPhereman made no movement. He took in the scene piece by piece. Detective Selmon went over to the porch and lead Malisha away from the crime scene. Most of all he didn't want any evidence destroyed. Other vehicles and police officials began pulling up at the crime scene. An ambulance and a forensic van parked along the curve.

Captain Mike Stanburg exited his vehicle followed by lieutenant Ashley Lopez and Tony Jones. McPhereman caught a glimpse of Fayetteville's elite and knew all reports would cross William Grey's desk. Being the lead detective, he took charge immediately.

"Okay! Let's get this crime scene taped off. I want a clear pathway for forensic officer Williams. Can you assist with that little girl so my partner can interview Ms. Mya 'Star' Davis? Thank you for your cooperation."

He made his way over to meet his superiors. Before he could extend his hand to greet the captain, Stanburg faced him in an irreverent manner, completely insidious. Noticing the way Stanburg's body language spoke he knew he had fucked up. "What happened here, detective?" Stanburg said. He had ascetic in his voice.

"Well, I only been on the scene for about 30 minutes, but so far we have a dead guy on the porch with several bullet holes in him. We have two eyewitnesses—the guy's mother and girlfriend. That's it so far."

"So, you don't have shit," Stanburg spoke formally. "Get this shit cleaned up immediately and keep out of the news reporter's face. I know they will be here soon. Mr. Grey will hear about this. I will personally see that he knows what a 'fine' job you are doing out here," Stanburg spoke with sarcasm.

Without another word, the elite turned toward their cars and left, leaving McPhereman speechless. Just when he thought things couldn't get any worse, a channel 11 news van pulled up.

CHAPTER 7

Trearina pulled up at the trap spot and cut the engine. Moments later her car was surrounded. She picked up her phone and called Pressure. He picked up on the first ring.

"Yo, who dis?"

"Nigga, you know damn well who this is, now get your little busted-ass friends from around my car."

"You better call next time."

"Whatever, nigga."

Pressure ended the call knowing it would piss her off. Pressure wanted to fuck Trearina but she wouldn't give him no play, so he got off by fucking with her. Pressure came out of the crib and niggas fell back, disappearing into the shadows of Grove View Terrace project.

Trearina got out of the car, slamming the car door behind her. She ran up on Pressure and started swinging. "Why the fuck you scare me like that?" Trearina was out of breath. "Damn! I got to stop smoking," she said, waiting to catch her breath.

Pressure took this moment to slide behind her. Damn, she got a nice ass, he thought. He drew back and slapped her across the ass. She came up swinging.

"Nigga, don't ever put your hands on me."

Pressure grabbed her and held her until she stopped fighting. He whispered in her ear, "When you gonna stop playing games and let me put a baby in you?"

She laughed at him. "Boy! Let me go." Pressure released his grip. She gave him the keyless remote to the Equinox but stopped in her tracks. She didn't have a way home. She was so caught up in Sunkist's instructions she forgot about herself. She pulled out her cell to call Sunkist. He didn't pick up, so she tried Fire. She didn't pick up. What the fuck, her last option was her baby's father. God knows she didn't want to ask that nigga for shit, but she didn't have a choice 'cause wasn't no Uber driver coming to the Grove View projects.

She dialed his number and waited for him to pick up. You got to be kidding me, she thought when he didn't pick up. She pushed her pride to the side. "Pressure! Can I just chill here tonight 'cause I'm tired and I just want to take a shower and go to sleep."

Pressure knew she had to be exhausted to request a sleepover in the trap. "You know I got you." Pressure put his arm around her neck and escorted her inside.

The apartment, to her surprise, was decked out. There was plush carpet on the floor and nice appliances. A new black sectional couch. A 65-inch flat screen hung from the wall. Y.G. and Grave-yard was playing Mortal Kombat on the PlayStation 5. They looked up from their entertainment briefly to see who walked in. Y.G. smirked and winked at Trearina before returning to his fun.

Pressure caught the little slick move Y.G. just pulled on Trearina. "Yo Y.G.! I ain't paying y'all to sit on y'all ass all night playing video games and shit. The work is in the whip outside. You and Grave-yard go handle that shit," Pressure demanded. Pressure threw the keyless remote to Y.G. He caught the remote. Him and Grave-yard headed for the door, but Pressure called Y.G. before he could make it out the door.

Y.G. stopped and looked over his shoulder. Pressure winked at him, returning the favor for him winking at Trearina. Y.G. stormed out the crib. Bitch-ass nigga always trying to show off for a bitch. Y.G. wasn't feeling the way Pressure played him.

Grave-yard thought the shit was funny. This was standup comedy at its best. Trearina couldn't help it, she was smiling from ear to ear.

"You want something to drink? I ain't got Silver Patron." He knew that was her favorite drink.

"Let me see what you got," she said. Trearina went over to the little mini bar. She was impressed at the wide range of champagne, Laurent-Perrier Cuvee Rose Maison, Crown Royal Canadian whisky, Remy Martin XO. "Hold on now, I got to try this Courvoisier XO cognac." She pulled the bottle from the rack.

Pressure pulled out two shot glasses from the cabinet and met Trearina at the kitchen table. She popped the bottle and sucked the suds away. Once the suds were gone, she poured their shots. She placed the bottle on the table. "No need for babysitting," Trearina said. She pinched her nose and threw her shot back. She held her breath and let the smooth liquor slide down her throat. She closed her eyes. She licked her lips, savoring the flavor.

Pressure was caught in her sex appeal. He forgot about his shot. She opened her eyes and to her surprise that nigga was just sitting there. "Oh, you playing games." Trearina took his shot and threw it back. Pressure wasn't really a drinker, but tonight, fuck it. He went to the cabinet and grabbed four more shot glasses. He lined them up on the table and filled every glass.

"Nigga, you not about that life," Trearina said. Pressure took a deep breath and exhaled. He picked up the first shot and downed it, simultaneously finishing the next four.

He slammed the glass on the table. "Catch up. Look like to me you running low on fuel." Trearina thought to herself, this nigga done bumped his head if he thinks he can outdrink me.

She lined the shot glasses up and filled them to the rim. She downed all five with no problem. "You out of your league, pretty boy." As the words came out of her mouth the impact hit her full force. Damn, that shit is strong. What they put in that shit, horse tranquilizers? Pressure just smiled at her and watched her transform.

The second wave that hit her came from the molly Pressure put in every bottle. She bit down on her lip, enjoying the sensation of the drug. She began rubbing her neck and caught herself. "Look, I'm 'bout to take a shower. Do you have anything I can sleep in?"

Trearina headed to the bathroom to take a shower. Once she was in the bathroom, she cut the shower on and adjusted the water temperature to her satisfaction. She slowly undressed. God, the cotton of her t-shirt felt so good against her skin. She sat on the edge of the tub and slid her pants off. The cool air sent chills up her spine. She removed her panties and felt her juices run down her leg. She ran her hand between her legs. The contact sent a bolt of electricity through her body almost knocking her off the tub. Her pussy began to throb for attention.

She leaned back against the shower wall and closed her eyes. She spread her legs and found her love button. She made circular motions with her finger on her clit. She slid her other two fingers inside her pussy. She began to moan with pleasure.

Click! The bathroom door opened. "All I could find was one of my tees." Trearina's mouth dropped to the floor. She was busted. Pressure played it off like he was shocked. Trearina looked around for something to cover herself. Pressure knew this was the moment he'd been waiting for. Trearina could see the hunger in his eyes. She closed her legs.

Pressure walked over to the tub and held out his hand. She accepted it and Pressure pulled her up and into his embrace. He knew she was vulnerable and wasted no time. He wrapped his arms around her and began kissing her on the neck. "Pressure, what are you doing? Can you please stop?"

She tried to push away in a useless attempt. Pressure found his way down to her left nipple. He licked the tip of her nipple and caressed the other one with his free hand. She was lost. One part of her wanted this but another part of her wanted to escape.

Pressure slid his tongue down to her navel. In one motion he lifted her off her feet and placed her on his shoulders. He pinned her against the wall. He palmed her ass and lifted her higher in the air. He began to eat her pussy and that's when she let go. She grabbed the back of his head and buried his face in her pussy. She rode his face. She placed one hand on the ceiling for support. "Mmm…oh, baby, right there."

Pressure could feel her legs shaking and knew she was about to cum. "Baby…baby…oh, shit…I'm 'bout to cum." Pressure sucked on her clit long and hard. She exploded all over his face. Pressure caught his breath while lowering her to the floor. She was still shaking from the orgasm.

"You okay?" Pressure asked. She didn't purposely reply. She turned her back to him and got in the shower.

Pressure admired her body as she walked toward the shower. Her body was flawless. Her skin was the color of brown sugar. She had a small waist and a fat ass. Her short hair added to her sex appeal. His appetite was impetuous when it came to her. He needed to be inside her. He got undressed. He slid the curtain back and joined her in the shower.

Trearina said nothing, she just let the water cascade down her body. He slid up behind her and wrapped his arms around her waist. She didn't resist his touch. He turned her around so she could face him. She slid her hand down his chest. He leaned down and kissed her passionately while gripping her ass. She let out a small moan.

He picked her up and she wrapped her legs around his waist. She wanted to use protection, but the head of his dick had already penetrated her. Pressure pushed himself further inside her until he felt her body tense up. She wrapped her arms around his neck and whispered in his ear, "Don't hurt me." They were bonded but the way she said don't hurt me woke up a beast.

He lowered her to her feet and turned her around so he could enter her from the back. She bent over and separated her feet perfectly apart. She placed both hands on the wall and looked back over her shoulder. She was ready.

He grabbed the back of her neck and with his other hand he gripped her waist. He slowly slid all the way inside her. She tried to run but there was nowhere to go. She cried out in pain and pleasure. He slid out of her slowly and began to long-dick her giving her all ten inches slow and steady. Her pussy muscles were gripping his dick. He didn't want to nut quick. Her pussy was good, and he wanted to enjoy this moment. He pulled out of her.

Trearina played with her clit. She wanted to let go of all her stress and in this indelible moment she was going to free herself. This was completely quintessential. After tonight there would be many ramifications, but she would deal with the consequences as they came.

He slid his dick down the crack of her ass. Trearina couldn't take it any longer. She reached between her legs and grabbed his dick. "Stop playing with me and fuck me like you love me." He slid back inside her with a purpose. With each thrust he lifted her off her feet, making sure she took every inch.

He slapped her ass as she screamed out. "Oh, God…hold on…shit."

"This what you want. Shut the fuck up and take this dick." He began to pump harder. All you could hear was her ass slapping against his midsection. He could feel the sensation building up in his body and knew he was getting ready to nut.

Trearina could feel the head of his dick growing. "Oh, baby… damn…don't…don't nut in me." She reached back, placing a hand on his stomach to slow his pace.

"Damn, you got some good pussy," his speech was slurred from the alcohol. Placing a hand on her back he pushed her down so she would arch her back and lift her ass. He gripped both sides of her hips so she couldn't run. He slammed into her with all his might. He wanted to touch the back of her throat if he could.

"Yes, baby…that's it right there." Her words drove him to driver deeper. "Oh, baby…I'm 'bout to cum." He speeded up the pace to catch up with her. "Fuck me harder…fuck me…." He felt himself about to explode.

"I'm cumming…oh, shit…oh, shit." With one deep, long stroke he busted inside her. His body jerked a couple of times as he filled Trearina up with cum.

Trearina snapped out of her emotional trance and came to reality. "What the fuck, nigga!" She pushed him off of her and ran to the toilet. She sat down and squeezed the cum out of her. "You must done lost your goddamn mind cumming in me. Do it look like I'm trying to get pregnant?"

Pressure wasn't trying to hear all that shit. He closed the curtain, cutting her off midsentence.

I know this nigga ain't just disrespected me after I just gave him some pussy. It's okay, though. He won't never touch me again. God, I feel fucking stupid. She was pissed, completely livid. She picked up her pants and took out her cell. She sent Sunkist a text: *Come get me now 911.* Within seconds her phone rang.

"What's good, you a'ight?"

"I'm at the trap spot in the Grove. I dropped that shit off and I'm ready to go."

"I'm on my way, but why you just now calling me?" The drop was over two hours ago.

"Nigga, I did call but I didn't get a answer."

Sunkist knew she was pissed about something. "A'ight, I'm on my way." Sunkist ended the call.

CHAPTER 8

"Hand me the scale, let me weigh this shit." Grave-yard handed Y.G. the scale. "Nigga, that's 36 ounces to the tee. I been hustling so long I can eye that shit and won't be off a gram," Grave-yard said.

"You ain't talking 'bout nothing. My nigga L. can step on this shit and bring back two babies and a lady," Y.G. proclaimed. They kept talking shit until the bathroom door opened.

Trearina came out and didn't say a word to them. She went and sat on the couch like she was waiting on somebody. Both hustlers bust out laughing 'cause they heard all the commotion coming from the bathroom. That's what your dumb ass get, bitch, Y.G. thought to himself.

Nineteen bricks sat on the counter. Grave-yard smiled to himself and began to rap. "I was standing in the kitchen over the stove, just water whip'n, mixing soda with the yoda, when it came to the coke game yo Gotti knew it best."

He went to the cabinet under the sink and pulled out four big silver pans. Perfect. He placed them on the top of the table. Let me see now…got to get the baking soda. Shit, fuck it. I'ma use dry baby laxative. He got his ingredients to cut the coke with and returned to the table. Y.G. joined him.

"Check this out. We gonna hit the coke with three ounces of cut for every ounce of coke."

"Move back, nigga. I see you don't know shit, li'l nigga." Grave-yard was a true chef when it came to the coke game. "Listen up and you may learn something. Grab me a brick and drop it in this pan."

Everybody froze in their tracks when the bathroom door opened. You could hear a rat piss on cotton it was so quiet. The atmosphere in the room was 50 below zero. "What the fuck y'all looking at? Y'all lost something over here?" Pressure wasn't feeling the vibe coming off of Y.G. and Grave-yard.

"It's your world, player, I'm just a squirrel trying to get a nut." Y.G. winked at him and got back to work.

Pressure grabbed the remote to the TV and cut it on. There were six different areas being monitored by camera. He clicked on camera one which viewed the front of the apartment building. He waited to see who exited the vehicle. After he saw Sunkist step out the car, he grabbed the four-channel radio and cleared the entrance, letting everyone that was under his leadership know that everything was good.

Pressure shot a look that could kill at Trearina, knowing the only way Sunkist would show his face and pull up at his spot was she called him. Pressure wasn't feeling this shit. He had the G for the streets and didn't need nobody checking him on his moves, not even Sunkist, who he was under.

Pressure looked closely at the screen and saw another fig-ure exiting the car. Sunkist knocked on the door. Trearina ran to the door to open it. She jumped into Sunkist's arms. "Damn! What took you so long?" she cried, kissing him on his cheek. She turned and gave Pressure a dissatisfying look. "I'll be in the car." She turned to leave and ran into Fire.

So, this was the reason he couldn't pick up when I called him, she thought. She played it cool though. "Hey, Unique," she spoke to Fire, calling her by her government.

"What's up, Tee?" Fire knew Trearina had a thing for Sunkist. She was just waiting on the day for her to cross them lines so she could fuck her ass up for being disloyal. Trearina was her best friend though, so she dropped the attitude and gave her best friend a hug.

"What is that on your shit?" Trearina was being her nosy self, Miss Private Investigator.

"Don't ask if you not trying to be involved in it." Knowing that it was blood on Fire's shirt, she put an end to her investigation.

"Well, look at the time, I'll be in the car." Everybody laughed at Trearina. They knew when it came to putting in work she was not about that life. Damn! That shit is strong as hell. Fuck COVID-19, this shit is gonna kill me. She pulled her mask up to block out the smell of the cocaine.

While Fire was talking, Sunkist was studious. Something just didn't sit right with him. Pressure kept avoiding eye contact, pretending to be preoccupied with work. Funny thing was, he didn't even salute him or Fire. Y.G. and Grave-yard acknowledged his presence with a head nod. They couldn't speak due to the masks covering their mouths.

Fire picked up on the vibe the atmosphere was giving off. She was the first to speak. Having general status, she moved like an O.G. The battleground was even since Pressure and Fire had the same rank inside their organization. She stepped in front of Sunkist. "Hi, homie," she said, giving her salute. "So, what we looking like over here?"

Pressure was impervious and his body language spoke insidiously. Shit! "We good over here, 20 birds ain't shit to deal with. I can have this shit gone by the end of the week, but shit, let's keep it gangsta. Why y'all pulling up on the trap now? Y'all ain't been pulling up, fucking with us."

Fire blinked her eyes a couple of times, letting Pressure's words sink in. When it finally registered, she flipped. "Nigga! Who the fuck you talking to? You sound like a bitch. What we got to come see you every day, hold your hand to show our love? Look around, nigga. Them 20 bricks is our shit. How many you buy? How many bands you put up for this shit? You need to get your priorities straight and start thinking with your head and not your dick. I'm a G homie, I can smell bullshit a mile away. You think Sunkist keep me under him because I'm another pretty face or that my pussy is good? Nah, nigga, I'm his third eye, I see all." Fire closed in on him. "That's my best friend, nigga. You don't think I know what's up?" She looked Pressure up and down with irreverence.

Pressure had enough of her mouth. Sunkist remained silent. Every man shows his true colors when money is involved or when a woman is involved. He let the scene play out. "Fire, you got me fucked up." Pressure could have snapped her neck. "I put more work in than any of these niggas. I make that shit disappear. You talking about y'all money like I ain't band up or something. Shit, if y'all feel some type of way there y'all bricks right there. Y'all can pack that shit up and catch the deuces."

Fire couldn't believe her ears after all the love they showed him. Now that he got his money, he wants to give them his ass to kiss. Fire was done talking. She wanted to put a bullet in his disloyal ass. Fire looked over at Sunkist with pleading eyes. She wanted him to give the okay and she was gonna show Pressure what the true meaning of a holy spirit is.

Sunkist stepped forward. "All that we do is not for selfish beneficial gain. If we took that course of action, we wouldn't have a foundation. There is no me, myself, and I on this team and if a nigga feel like that they was never a part of this team. We make sure our family eat. Niggas behind the wall need appeal lawyers, JPays, cash apps. Police on our payroll got to get paid. Nigga got to make bond. Who you think make that shit happen? We do. No one person in this room moves this team but me. If you want to go your own way, a bullet marks the X."

Sunkist pulled his XD-40 followed by Fire, Y.G. and Grave-yard. Pressure took a deep breath and exhaled. "I mean, since y'all put it that way." Sunkist just dropped his head.

Fire cracked a smile. "This nigga!" Y.G. and Grave-yard placed their pistols back in their waistline.

Sunkist knew Pressure better than anybody in the crew. Pressure only respected pressure. You have to match him on the same level or he took you for weak. "Now that we got that out the way, what we looking at," Sunkist said, rubbing his hands together.

"A'ight, big homie, dis what's up. The coke good as fuck so I can really step on this shit but I'm not going to max it out though. Out of these 20 I'm bring back 35 with no problem. Fuck flying south, these birds flying west for the summer. I got Lil Y.G. in here taking history lessons on this shit."

"A'ight, that's good news 'cause I'm going to cop 50 next time, so let these birds fly. Pressure, you holla at the homies in Rocky Mount?"

"Yeah, the nigga smack on the yard so I holla at Lil Don. You talking 'bout the young hog Hue?"

"Yeah, that's him. Yeah, I met cuz when I was at Bertie a couple years back."

Sunkist knew Lil Don well and thought to himself. He did need a standup nigga to push to for the Rocky Mount and Tarboro area and Lil Don was just the guy. He kept a mental note. Sunkist glanced at his Omega 007 edition Rolex. It read 3:10 a.m. "A'ight, y'all nigga take care of business and keep me up to date on shit. Oh yeah, before I go, y'all know that nigga William Grey?"

"Yeah, you talking about the chief of police, right?"

"Yeah, that nigga. A'ight, y'all know that we got Lt. Ashley Lopez on the payroll, so this nigga sent word to me through her that it's time to break bread."

What! He tired us like that. The steam was rolling off Fire's neck. "Shit! Let's get his ass missing, you know that's my specialty."

"Grave-yard got his name from the bodies he laid in their final resting spot. It's not that easy as it may seem, his connections run deep. It's hard to kill the head when the body got many arms, but in due time Grave-yard will add him to his collection." With that said, Fire and Sunkist left the apartment. When they got in their vehicle Trearina was fast asleep. Fire hit the push-to-start and pulled off into the night.

CHAPTER 9

Angel stepped out of her pearl white 2021 Toyota Camry. She closed her door and hit her alarm. The sky was clear and the sun hid behind the clouds. The temperature was in the low 80s. Angel had her hair down. She sported a Tom Ford wraparound dress that hugged her hips just right. The purple dress matched her Dolce & Gabbana heels. Clutched to her side was a Bottega Veneta handbag. She rocked Johnny Nelson earrings and a Rolex Submariner purple face to glorify her outfit. Looking and smelling like a million bucks, she made her way inside Cross Creek Mall.

She wanted to grab a couple of items that she could dress in so she wouldn't look like money. She had a long way to go in the transformation of downsizing from what she was used to. She was used to spending her daddy's money and not her own. Now that she was paying her own bills and had to provide for herself, she had to manage her money.

She crossed the food court, smelling and viewing all the types of food that were on display. A small Asian woman approached her and asked if she wanted to try some pepper chicken. She declined the offer.

"Damn, baby girl. What's your name?" She turned around to see who was speaking to her.

"My name is job, education, and stability. What's your name?" Angel stood there with her hand on her hips waiting on a reply. He was caught completely off guard.

"I just think you are fine, and I wanted to get to know you."

"Well, thank you for not trying to spit no lame-ass game but I'm not looking to be involved with anyone right now, but it was nice to meet you." Without saying another word, she left him standing there, making sure to put more sway in her hips as she walked away. He watched her until she vanished into the flow of shoppers.

The letters D.T.L.R. caught her attention and she went inside. A brown skinned female with a short cut greeted her. "Welcome to D.T.L.R., my name is Regina. If there is anything I can help you with just let me know."

She nodded her head. After picking through a couple of clothes racks she came across a black and pink shirt with the words "EAT ME" across the front in pink letters. Now, let me find some jeans to match. She picked a pair of midnight black Michael Kors denim jeans. Perfect, she thought.

She headed to the shoe section. Picking up a pair of black and pink Air Max 95 sneakers, it was love at first sight. She took her merchandise to the checkout counter. Waiting for the cashier to give her her total, she took out her cell and sent her high school friend Unique a text. "I'm in the Ville now and haven't seen you yet. I'm going to the Big Apple tonight. Come and turn up with me." She hit send and placed her phone back in her bag.

Angel and Unique had been best friends when they grew up in Alabama. They did everything together but after they graduated Unique married and moved away. Even though they went their separate ways they always stayed in contact. Now that she had moved to Fayetteville she couldn't wait to see Unique in person.

"That will be $220.94. Will you paying cash or card?"

"Oh, that will be card." Angel gave the cashier her card.

"Thank you for your purchase and please come again." The cashier bagged her merchandise and handed it to her.

She left the store as her phone alerted her that she had a message. She decided to grab something to eat and headed for the food court. Watching the little Asian woman cater to the crowd made her smile. "May I try some, miss?" The little Asian woman was excited that she came back. The little Asian woman handed her the pepper chicken on a little stick. She popped it in her mouth and waited for the spices to hit her taste buds. The soft chicken and flavor left her mouth watering for more. "Okay, you got me. Let me get a plate to go." The Asian woman smiled with joy and requested Angel's order.

Angel sat and waited at a nearby table while her order was placed. Let me check my messages while I'm waiting. She saw Unique had texted her back and agreed to go to the Big Apple with her tonight. She texted Unique her address and told her to be ready by 9:00.

Her food was ready. After paying for her food, she left the mall.

The black, polished Bentley GT Continental came to a stop in front of the two-story mansion. The driver parked and got out to open the door for William Grey. "Have a great day."

He was dressed in a six-button Versace Royal suit. The suit was a midnight blue with a sky blue inside vest. Shoes were Ferragamo custom to his feet. Watch was Cartier with an ocean blue face and sky blue band. He made his way to the mansion's front door, leaving a trail of fragrance, Acqua di Gio by Giorgio Armani.

He rang the doorbell. After about a two-minute wait, an intercom came on. "The mayor will see you now."

The door clicked. He turned the knob and entered the house. A white woman in her late 50s greeted him and escorted him to the mayor's chambers. The escort knocked on the mayor's door and waited to gain entrance. "Come in," Mr. James Peterson said in his raspy voice.

Mayor James Peterson was a pioneer in the game. He was in his early 50s and was taught the game at an early age. Making money made his dick hard. He was the plug and with his seat at the high table he was not only invincible but also invisible. He was turning the game over to Grey. Grey was his protégé and over the years he taught him well. He connected Grey with some of the most influential people on the east coast. With this move and with Grey under his wing, he became legendary.

Grey entered the room. The office was old-fashioned, not even a phone was in the room. This room was specialized for meetings. The room was soundproof. No one could hear in or out. There was a device that cut off any telecommunication signal.

Peterson stood and shook Grey's hand. "Please have a seat." Peterson motioned with his hand that everything was okay, and the escort closed the office door.

Grey reached into his jacket and pulled out a white envelope and handed it to Peterson. "Thank you. I see things are going as planned."

"Everything is good, and business is okay."

Peterson noticed the choice of words that Grey chose to use. Peterson repeated the sentence. "Business is okay…. So, tell me Mr. Grey, why business is not great."

"Our product is moving at a slower pace than our number one competition but I'm having that problem taken care of as we speak."

"That's good news, Mr. Grey. There will be 100 keys arriving this Wednesday in Port City. I will give you notice of what dock number to pick them up at. Good day to you." Peterson stood and hit the button under his desk. Two guards opened the office doors to escort Mr. Grey back to his car.

Once he was outside, he got in his car and left. He pulled out his cell to call Captain Mike Stanburg. He picked up on the second ring.

"Before you ask, our agent is all over it. We have the files on Corey Adams aka Pressure, Unique Spellman aka Fire, Trearina McNeil aka Tee, and Javier Green aka Grave-yard. We have a confidential informant inside their organization. We are trying to find the whereabouts of Joel Smith aka Sunkist before we make our move, plus we want to catch them with the drugs. That's more money in our pockets."

"I just left the mayor and I assured him that this problem would be handled accordingly. I want these motherfuckers in a grave or in jail. Fuck the extortion plan, we got 100 bricks on the way. Call me when the job is done." Grey ended the call.

CHAPTER 10

"Baby, you want some breakfast?" Fire stood over Sunkist, shaking him trying to wake him up.

"O.M.G. babe, we just got in around 4:30 this morning, let a nigga rest."

"Okay, cool but your mama downstairs."

Sunkist jumped out of bed. What the fuck she doing here and how she get the address? Unique stood there in her booty shorts with a smile on her face. "I knew that would get your ass up."

"Oh, you want to play, huh?"

Unique ran to the other side of the bed, blocking Sunkist's path. Sunkist jumped over the bed and grabbed her. He picked her up and slammed her onto the bed. He picked up one of the pillows and smacked her upside the head with it. She kicked him in the chest, flipping him out of bed. Oh shit! She heard a thud on the floor. "Are you okay?" she said, peaking over the side of the bed.

As soon as she was in his sight, he grabbed her arm and slid her off the bed onto the floor. He got between her legs and pinned her down to the floor so she couldn't move. She fought under his weight, but it was useless. He laughed at her. "I hate you," she smiled.

Sunkist loosened his grip and she used it to flip him onto his back. She sat on top of him. "You slippin' on your pimping, player." They both laughed. He palmed her ass. Just the touch of her skin made his dick hard. She smelled so good. He pulled her in and kissed her passionately. She moaned under his embrace and slid her hand inside his boxer shorts and caressed his manhood. Once her fingers felt the full length of him, she slid his dick out of hiding.

They locked eyes as she slid down his chest. She took the head of his dick and licked around it. He closed his eyes, enjoying the moment. This was the first time she gave him head. She licked up and down his shaft while jacking him at a slow speed. Once he felt her mouth enclose on his dick, he let out a long moan of satisfaction. He slid his hands in her dreads, guiding the motion. He opened his eyes.

She slid down his shaft, taking in his whole dick. His toes curled as his dick slid down her throat. "Oh my God, baby… what the fuck." Sunkist gripped her dreads from the sensation. She did something with her throat that almost made him nut in her mouth. She came up and swallowed him again. This time she didn't let go. With the full length of his dick in her mouth she began to suck with the back of her tongue. "Baby, I'm 'bout to nut…oh shit." She sucked harder as he exploded in her mouth. She swallowed every drop.

Sunkist laid there catching his breath. "You want some breakfast now?" she said with a smile.

"Hell yeah. While you at it, let me get two cups of orange juice." They both laughed. Sunkist went to take a shower. Unique went to fix their plates. Fifteen minutes later Sunkist was out the shower. Let me see what I want to wear today. The head game that Unique just gave him left an indelible memory plus that shit had his swag on a 100.

Time to get fresh. He chose a pair of Dior black shorts, a black and white Y.S.L. belt. He chose a simple white wife beater and a pair of black, white, and red Jordan 6s. He checked himself out in the mirror and thought inadvertently that this outfit ain't complete. What was missing…oh, that's what's missing.

He picked up a bottle of Polo Red by Ralph Lauren. He hit his neck, chest, and opened his shorts to refresh his privates. Now I'm complete. He made his way down the steps and into the kitchen.

Unique and Trearina were sitting at the table deep in girl talk when he entered. "Good morning, ladies. What's on y'all agenda for today? Me personally, I got to go pick my kids up from my mama house since somebody let me fall asleep in the car last night."

At that moment Fire's phone alerted her she had a text message. I wonder who that is. She picked up her phone and unlocked it. "Oh shit, my homegirl is in town and want me to go to the Big Apple tonight with her."

"Your homegirl who?" Trearina's private-eye mode kicked in. "Because last time I checked, I was the only homegirl you got."

"Her name is Angel, we grow up together, but when I moved from Alabama we didn't kick it as much 'cause of the long distance. I got to find something to wear."

Unique was excited and it showed all in her facial expressions. Sunkist hadn't seen her this happy in awhile, so he was cool with her hanging out with her friend. Sunkist knew how Fire's mind worked. She was a flower that needed the sun and the rain. She was loyal, death before dishonor. If she embraced you, she would die for you. There was no borderline with her. If she fucked with you there were no limits. If she didn't fuck with you, she wouldn't even speak.

Sunkist never completely understood how he pulled her to know her story. She didn't even fuck with niggas but chose him. I guess real recognizes real.

"I guess I got to find something to get into tonight." His phone rang. He looked at the incoming call. Who the fuck calling from a 252? He answered the call.

"You have a prepaid call from Boss Loc, an inmate at Bertie Correctional Institution. This call will be monitored and recorded. If you choose to accept the call, press five now." Sunkist accepted the call. "Thank you for using Global Tellink."

"What's cracking, cuz?"

"Not shit, groove. Moving and grooving. Yo homie, I need like $250 to get online. Nigga got a beat the boss already activated."

"What you need, a Western Union or cash app?"

"You can do a cash app to $lilsody83. You already know the name."

"A'ight, I'm 'bout to do it now."

"A'ight, good look, homie."

"That shit done, cuz."

"Oh yeah, before I forget, Treys-Up sends his love."

"Fo sho, cuz. I wrote the homie's crime boss and told him to give my info to cuz. You know I was at Caledonia before I came home. I left the homies a phone but I ain't heard from them. Shit might got knocked off. What's up with Ace? I heard the fed got him and baby Ace," said Sunkist.

"Hell yeah, shit crazy right now, but if you hear from 54 West tell him to pull up on me."

"I got you, cuz. Is cuz still fucking with J-Roc? 'Cause I know a lot of them neighborhood niggas pushing with Father."

"I don't know, cuz. Shit! Holla at Big Gum."

"A'ight then, cuz. I'm 'bout to handle some business. I'll holla back at you." Sunkist ended the call.

CHAPTER 11

"Amanda Koontz, are you ready to proceed?" The judge was trying to wrap up his last case so he could go home. He glanced at his watch: 4:40. He just shook his head and waited patiently on the district attorney.

Koontz was flipping through the defendant file trying to find his prior conviction sheet. Got it! "Your honor, the defendant is a record level six. At this time the state is requesting that the bond be raised to $500,000 cash to assure the defendant with out-of-state criminal charges be present in court."

"Would the defendant's attorney like to speak before I make a final determination?"

"Yes, your honor. My client has a citation in Harnett County with no other pending charges. Mr. Patrick Young has turned himself in of his own free will. There is no need to revoke his bond, especially since Mr. Young is an undercover confidential informer working with law enforcement to reduce his charges. Let me remind Ms. Koontz that interfering with an ongoing operation that could lead to the arrest of Cumberland County's most dangerous criminal organizations wouldn't be a wise move."

The district attorney gathered her things and walked out of the courtroom knowing she had lost.

"I will let the bond stay the same due to the defendant's co-operation with law enforcement. Mr. Young, you are free to go."

He shook his lawyer's hand and was out the door. Damn, it sure felt good getting the fuck out of there. The air even felt different. A black Crown Vic pulled up to the curb. Damn, they on my ass. He opened the door and got in.

"How did court go?" Stanburg adjusted the sleeves on his Valentino shirt.

"It went good and the lawyer you sent to represent me was a beast. Thank you for that shit, word up."

"That's good to hear that things worked out for you. Me and Roy go way back, so when I asked him to represent you it was free of charge. You know how things go—one hand washes the other. Now, tell me what you got for me."

"A'ight, so, this nigga got the streets on lock and I'm not talking 'bout Fayetteville. The streets respect the nigga 'cause he is a standup dude, something that money can't buy, so his connections run from the streets of North Carolina to the flat lands on the west coast. Even the niggas and officers behind the wall fuck with this nigga."

"See, y'all think the money is coming from drug money. No! It's coming from business people that ain't have a pot to piss in and now they are C.E.O.s of their own companies. The drug money is a tool to capitalize and be a part of the American dream. He never has drugs around him so it's going to be hard catching him with anything. Second, it's going to be hard knowing his whereabouts. The nigga move like a ghost and nobody know where he stay or lay his head."

Captain Stanburg contemplated on the knowledge he just obtained. His blood was boiling. He grabbed the young thug by his throat. "You listen to me, and you listen to me good. I don't give a fuck if you got to fuck him and fall in love to gain his trust, you get me something that I can use to put him and them criminals away for good or your ass is going to prison, and I will make sure personally that everyone knows that you are a rat. You got that?" He snatched Young's chain off his neck. "Get the fuck out."

Young opened the door and got out, slamming the door behind him. The Crown Vic pulled off.

CHAPTER 12

"Cuz, look! Damn! She fat to death." Boo let down his window. "Yo, all y'all lawyers built like that? If so, I'm trying to build a case right now."

Crimz was in the driver seat shaking his head and laughing at his homeboy.

Koontz stopped in her tracks after hearing someone being disrespectful. "Are you talking to me?" she frowned.

"Nah, I'm talking to the lady behind you." Boo smirked with his comment.

Okay, we can play this game. She walked over to their car. "So, what's your name, handsome?" She turned on her sex appeal. Being Hispanic she had a natural beauty.

Crimz was the first to speak. My name is Dy'Shawn.

"You mean Mr. Dy'Shawn Wilson, 29 years of age, staying at 1141 Brookstore apartments?"

Crimz was dumbfounded. Boo looked over at Crimz, "You know this chick?"

"Hell nah, I don't know her."

"That's what I thought. Don't come asking for some shit you really don't want. For the record, my name is Amanda head-district-attorney Koontz." She turned and walked off, leaving them speechless.

"Damn, my nigga, what the fuck just happen?"

"I don't know, but Tee-Tee need to bring his ass out that courthouse so we can get the fuck out of here."

Three minutes later Tee-Tee came swagging out the court like he owns Cumberland County.

"Nigga, bring your ass on, you ain't have shit but a ticket. You acting like you beat trial."

Tee-Tee hopped in, and they pulled off. "Yo, ain't that the nigga who runs with Pressure? I think he fucks with Mia that stays on the westside."

"Yeah, that's him, but what the fuck he getting out of a D.T. car, man? That shit don't look right, homie."

Boo pulled out his phone and called Pressure. After four rings he got the voicemail. He ended the call and sent Pressure a text: Holla at me a.s.a.p. He slid his phone in his pocket.

"What y'all getting into tonight?" Crimz said, maneuvering through traffic.

"The Big Apple 'pose to be jumping tonight and you know the hoes is gonna be out there."

"Sit back, little nigga, you can't even get in, especially with that baby face."

Boo was picking on Tee-Tee. Even though Tee-Tee was 25 he looked like he was 17. "Fuck you. I bet I'll be up in your bitch tonight. Don't leave your girl around me…true player for real."

"Oh, you Usher now?" they busted out laughing.

"So, what's the plan? We gonna meet up out there?"

"Shit, it don't matter," Crimz said, eyeing a little light skinned shorty in a red Honda.

"Cool with me. A'ight bet then." Boo's phone rang. He looked at the caller ID and saw it was Pressure.

"What's good, my nigga?" asked Pressure

"Yo homie, I just left the courthouse and seen your boy getting out a undercover car."

"My boy who?"

"That nigga Y.G."

"Nigga, what! A'ight fo sho, homie, 'preciate."

Boo ended the call.

CHAPTER 13

Fire stepped out of the shower. The smell from Herbal Essences shampoo filled the room. She sat on the edge of the California king-size bed to apply her Suave body lotion. Tonight she was gonna turn up with Angel. I know this bitch gonna be on her shit tonight. She thought about what she was gonna wear. She had been waiting to sport the outfit Sunkist got her for her birthday. She wanted to wait and wear it on a special occasion with him. Tonight called for extreme measures, and this would be that special occasion.

She could kill two birds with one stone, she thought. I could have a great night out with my friend and then come back and make love to the man I finally chose to give my heart. She was celibate and if it was up to her no nigga would ever enjoy the paradise that lay between her legs.

She viewed herself in the full-length mirror. Damn, I'm a bad bitch. She turned to view herself from the back. She slid her hands down her curves. She wiggled her butt awhile, biting down on her bottom lip. Should I really give him this good-good, she smiled, being silly.

Her smile slowly faded. She was 28 years of age. She hadn't had sex in close to seven years. She slid her finger between her pussy lips and tasted herself. Sweet! She thought, walking over to the dresser. Nothing but Victoria's Secret. She took out a bra and panty set, popped the tag, and put them on.

Now, let's see what type of mood am I in? Fuck your best friend mood? Nah. She declined the Gucci memoire. I want to get pregnant mood? Yesss. She chose the fragrance Sauvage by Dior and applied it. Let's get these lips right. She chose a gloss by Chanel Paris. She popped her lips a couple times. Finished.

Since her dreads came to her shoulders, she chose to let them hang naturally. Now, time to set this shit off. She thought about the Lil Boosie song "Set It Off." She hummed the song as she went to her closet.

Her phone rang. She ran to receive the call, knowing it was Angel. "Hello!"

"What's up, girl? You getting ready?"

"Bitch, you know what's up. Give me about 15 minutes and I'll be ready."

"Okay, cool. Do you want me to pick you up or do you want to drive?"

"You can come…" Unique thought about how Sunkist would feel if she told Angel to come to the crib. "Matter fact, I'ma drive, I'm too hype to be a passenger. This our night. We got to make up for lost time."

"Okay then, I'm heading out there now, but I'ma wait in my car until you pull up, okay?"

"A'ight! See you in a little bit." Fire ended the call. She looked at the time on her phone. It read 8:20. She threw her phone on the bed and ran back to her closet. She grabbed her PH5 dress and a pair of Femme LA 169 shoes. She got dressed.

Standing in the mirror she made sure when she stepped out heads were gonna turn. Satisfied with her appearance, she grabbed her phone, keys, and purse and was out the door. She hit the alarm on her CLK Mercedes.

She sent a text to Sunkist letting him know that she was leaving to join her friend Angel at the Big Apple. She sent another text to Angel saying she was on her way.

Sunkist texted back, "Have fun and enjoy yourself, love."

She whispered to herself, "love you too."

She put her phone in her dash holder. "Alexa, find a list of Lil Baby songs." She tapped on the first song on the list.

"I'ma turn up on a hater every chance that I get." As the lyrics flowed through her speakers, she hit her sound switch and heard the two 15-inch subs she had in her trunk kick in. She threw on her Gucci shades and pulled off. Twenty minutes later she pulled up at the Big Apple.

The club parking lot was packed. She chose to park at the gas station across the street. Once she parked, she texted Angel and told her she was here and to meet her in line. She made her way across Yadkin Road. She saw Angel getting out of her Toyota Camry. "Over here, girl…over here."

"I see you, girl." Angel shut her car door. Once her car was secured, she ran towards Fire. "What's up, girl?"

Angel jumped into Fire's arms. "You ready to turn up?"

"Hell yeah, bitch, let's go." They walked hand in hand until they reached the back of the line.

"Damn, this shit long as fuck," Angel said, looking at the distance to the club entrance.

Fire pulled out her cell and texted Sunkist: "Baby, do you know anybody at the Big Apple that will get us into the VIP and out of this long-ass line?" She waited for a minute but there was no text back.

"Oh my God, it's hot out here," Angel whined.

"Yo! Fire." She could hear somebody calling her name, so she stepped to the side of the line to see who it was. The bouncer was motioning her to come to the front of the line.

She grabbed Angel's hand. "Come on, girl."

They made their way to the front of the line. "What the fuck?"

"Oh, hell no."

"Man, we been out this bitch for 20 minutes."

Fire smiled to herself hearing people complaining about them breaking the line. Big Tank opened the door for the ladies. "This is complimentary from Sunkist," Big Tank said, closing the door behind Angel and Fire.

"Come on, girl, let's hit the bar and see what they got." Fire led the way. There were two white girls posted up at the bar. She was kind of cute, but the other one looked like the bouncer that just let them in. "What you want to drink, Angel?"

"Let me get that Grey Goose France."

The lady behind the bar was mixed, maybe Asian and black. She looked young. "Coming right up," the bartender announced.

"Make that two," Fire said, giving Angel a smile.

The bartender poured their drinks and handed them to them. They wasted no time. They threw their shots back and gave each other a high five. "Let me get two bottles of that Grey Goose, what you say, Angel, France?"

She laughed. At that moment two brothers pulled up to the bar. "How y'all ladies doing tonight?"

Fire scanned the brother from head to toe. Saint Laurent shirt, Tom Ford pants, and Stacy Adams shoes. Cartier Crash watch and a small gold chain. He was deep, dark chocolate with grey eyes and a bald head. She chose to speak.

"We are doing fine, and yourself?"

"Doing a lot better now that I'm in your presence."

Fire broke eye contact with the gentleman. "I'm sorry, where are my manners? This is my girlfriend Angel." Angel gave a shy smile as she was being introduced.

"Oh, y'all are together?"

"But of course," Fire pulled Angel closer to her.

"Okay then, ladies, y'all have a nice night." The brothers left.

Angel busted out laughing. "Girl, you still up to your old tricks."

"Best believe it."

They found a table in the corner away from the crowd. Fire sat the bottle on the table. "We forgot our shot glasses."

"I'm 'bout to go get some." Angel headed to get the shot glasses. Fire took her seat and waited for Angel to return.

Fire was grooving to the music when she saw a group of girls come her way. Fire slid her hand in her purse and got her straight razor just in case these bitches had something on their mind. As they got closer, she knew two of the girls.

Star, Shay, and Mia were the first three to approach the table, followed by Meme and Nikki. Star was the H.N.I.C. in their clique, so she took the initiative. "What's up with this shit I'm hearing that your nigga had my baby daddy killed?"

Fire stood up calmly and walked around the table to face Star. "Look, I don't know where you got your information, but if my nigga wanted your baby daddy dead, he wouldn't send a nigga to do it, he would kill that bitch nigga himself."

Star had heard and seen Fire in action and knew she wasn't nothing to play with, but the thought of her baby daddy lying in blood made every demon inside her respond to Fire's disrespect-ful-ass mouth. Star got in Fire's face. "Bitch, if I find out…."

Mia stepped between the two females. She knew she couldn't let no harm come to Fire due to her nigga Y.G. being a part of their organization. At that moment Angel approached the table. "Yo, what's up? Why you in my girl face like that?" Angel stepped in front of Fire.

"Yo, what the fuck y'all got going on with my people?" Crimz said walking up, followed by Boo and Tee-Tee.

Star looked around, sizing up the situation. She took a deep breath and exhaled. "Fuck this shit. My baby daddy didn't bleed pussy and I'm not either. This bitch Fire got some motherfuckin' explaining to do."

Angel stepped aside knowing her friend. Fire picked up the bottle of Grey Goose and smacked Star in the head with it. "Who the fuck you think you talking to, hoe?" Fire gripped her by the hair and punched her in the mouth. "When you see a gangsta like me, you salute me."

"Get the fuck off of her." Nikki slapped Fire and rushed her. Both females fell to the floor. Meme and Shay ran over and started kicking Fire. Mia just stood there. Angel ran over to the table and grabbed the other bottle of Grey Goose. She looked from Meme to Shay. She drew the bottle back and cracked it over Shay's head.

Shay screamed out in pain. Fire grabbed Meme's foot and cut her across the stomach. Once she fell, Fire grabbed her by the hair and began to cut her face up with the straight razor. Star finally got to her feet.

Bouncers came from everywhere. They broke the fight up. Once the fight was over one of the bouncers called an ambulance for Meme, Shay, and Star. Big Tank escorted Fire and Angel out the side door. He made sure they got safely to their cars.

Angel got in her car as Fire crossed over Yadkin Road to get her car. Fire sat in her car until Angel pulled up beside her. Angel parked, got out of her car, and got in with fire. "You good, sis?" Angel asked.

Fire was checking herself out in the rearview mirror. "Yeah, I'm good. Thanks for having my back in there."

"You know I got you. What are friends for? What the hell was that about, though? I mean, I left to get the shot glasses and when I came back all hell had broke loose."

"Shit, them bitches acting like they wanted smoke, so I gave them Fire."

"You know they ain't got that gangsta shit in them," Angel said, putting on her gangsta grill.

Fire's phone rang. She glanced at her phone to see who was calling. Fuck! It was Sunkist. He must have heard what jumped off. Motherfuckers just can't keep their mouths shut. Might as well get it over with. "Hey, babe, we leaving the club now."

"So, you gonna act like you ain't just crack a bitch over the head with a Grey Goose bottle? Big Tank put me on game, but you a'ight though?"

"Yeah, I'm good but damn, we wasn't in the club 20 minutes before that shit jumped off. That bitch Star pulled up on me talking stupid, talking 'bout you had her baby daddy killed…."

Fire knew she was slipping letting that type of information come out of her mouth over the phone, plus in the presence of anyone outside her organization. She peaked over at Angel. Angel was tuned into her phone. "Baby, we'll talk some more when I get home."

"A'ight, cool. I'm 'bout to meet up with Pressure now. He said it was important. Oh yeah, your twin is coming down from New York. She heard what happen in the club."

"No, she ain't heard shit, your ass called and told her what the fuck happen. Man, I'ma talk to you later."

She hung up the phone. She leaned forward and put her head on the steering wheel. "Why would he tell my sister that shit knowing how she is gonna respond?"

"You talking 'bout Zionna?" Angel said, pushing her phone aside.

"Yes, girl."

Angel had never met Zi in person, but she remembered hearing stories about her. She heard lately that she had left North Carolina and went to New York and became a queen-pin. Angel knew that Zi had a street credibility that went into the hall of fame.

"Angel, we just gonna call it a night. All this shit done stressed me the fuck out."

"That's okay, we can get together any day now that I'm down here for good. I'll hit you up tomorrow to check and see if you are okay." Angel leaned over and hugged Fire.

"Okay, girl, see you tomorrow."

Angel got out and Fire pulled off. On the way home, Fire's mind was everywhere. She hadn't seen her sister in two years. Zionna Smith aka Zi was her twin. You couldn't tell them apart when they were younger growing up in the Bam. They had to wear different hair styles or paint their fingernails different so people could set them apart. The only one that immediately could pick them apart was their mother.

Fire never wanted this type of lifestyle. She damn sure played the cards she was dealt and didn't blink an eye. Fire thought her life would consist of a husband, kids, and a big house to raise them in. A garden in the backyard where she would plant some vegetables, maybe some tomatoes, squash, and peppers. She wanted to become a L.P.N. so she could help people. Now she was helping people to an early grave, the complete opposite of what she wanted out of life.

She blamed her sister for transforming her into the person she was today, but that was a double-edged sword because without her transformation she would still be dumb, deaf, and blind. She was considered to be an 85 percenter without knowledge of self. The game was to be sold, not to be told. Her sister showed her the ins and outs from pimping to robbing, from shooting dice to shoplifting. The more she learned the more she became fascinated, especially being taught by her role model.

When she first met Sunkist, he was dead broke hustling merchandise out at the Bragg Flea Market. Her and her sister were out shopping and thought to stop by and pay their friend Peaches a visit at the flea market. They spent some money at the outside tables just to give back to the community. They came to a table where everybody was crowded around buying stuff. Sunkist was moving back and forth from customer to customer. Zi watched him collect $400 within 20 minutes and knew she had to have him on her team.

They approached his table. "Hey ladies, how are y'all do today?" He was counting his money while passing a customer their bag. He hadn't even looked in their direction yet, moving to the next two customers. When he finished he finally looked their way. "Sorry to keep y'all waiting. Do y'all see anything y'all like?"

Fire couldn't break her stare. He was the finest dude she ever saw in her life. Zi spoke first. "Yeah, there is something that I like and it's...." Before she could finish her sentence Fire bumped her with her shoulder, knowing that Zi was about to holla at him. Zi already had a nigga, so he would be just a little play toy.

Never seeing Fire wanting to talk to a dude, Zi stepped aside. Fire pretended to be interested in an iPhone case that wouldn't even fit her iPhone. "How much you want for this phone case?"

"I'll let it go for 20."

"I'll give you 15 for it."

"The price is 20."

I know he didn't. Fire put the phone case down and turned to leave.

"I tell you what, I'll let you get it on a discount."

She stopped and turned back around. "And what's the discount?" Fire said, placing her hand on her hip, poking her lips out.

"I'll take off $5 for that beautiful smile, and I'll take off another five if you will let me take you out to eat."

She blushed and smiled. "Okay, you got a deal." She paid for the case, gave him her number, and the rest was history.

Since Zi had North Carolina on lock she wanted to expand. She taught Sunkist the game and gave him a million dollar phone with all her North Carolina connections. This was a gift to him and her sister. Seeing that Sunkist wasn't your normal 'hood nigga, she knew he had the potential to be something great. Plus, with his skills, intelligence, and fearless demeanor they would capitalize in this world. She introduced Sunkist to NappBasher and Sunkist became family. Now she was coming back to the Ville and all Fire could do was shake her head as she drove home.

CHAPTER 14

Lil Don pulled up in the Ville around 6 p.m. Wednesday afternoon. The sun was out, a high in the mid-80s. As he drove down Ramsey Street, he kept glancing at the GPS so he would know where to make his next turn.

"Make a left onto Grove Street and your destination will be on your left." Listening to the GPS, he followed the directions. He soon pulled up into the Grove View Apartments.

Shit didn't look the same from the last time he was down here. He looked at the apartment sign as he drove past. Cape Fear Apartments. Damn, they done remodeled this shit. He drove to the back of the apartments and parked. There were about 20 niggas posted up looking in his direction. Man, let me call this nigga before I have to put a hole in one of these niggas.

He pulled his Nina and sat it on his lap. He called Pressure. He picked up immediately. "Yo, I seen you when you pulled up. I already holla at Sunkist and he said give you four of them things. Just sit right there, the homie Killa 'bout to pull up on you." Pressure ended the call.

Moments later Killa pulled up beside him and handed him four bricks in a brown paper bag. Killa pulled off, leaving just as quick as he came.

Lil Don checked the product and was satisfied. He texted Sunkist, confirming that he received his order. He pulled out of the projects and headed back to Rocky Mount.

Y.G. was in the back seat of a rented Ford Escape recording the transaction between Killa and Lil Don. After reviewing the footage, he downloaded the video and sent a copy to Stanburg. He called Stanburg.

"I just sent you a video and the nigga that picked the drugs up is pulling out of the projects now. He is in a white Charger with black stripes on the hood."

"Thank you, Mr. Young. I will have all units on it."

Y.G. hung up. Y.G. headed back to Enterprise to turn the rental in and get his car back. After switching cars, he called Pressure. "What's good, homie? Where you at?"

"We all going over to mama house now to drop off her presents. After we drop my mama presents off we going over to the basement to drop a couple of bars in the sound booth over at D.J. Black's crib."

"Word! You know I got to pull up."

"Shit, meet us over there then."

"A'ight. Peace!"

Pressure ended the call and called Sunkist. "Hey homie, what the business is? I'm 'bout to pull up on you now."

"Good, 'cause you know them Meadow Woods niggaz Boo, Crimz, and Tee-Tee?"

"Yeah, I know them niggaz, what about them though?"

"Shit! They got smoke."

"Nah, ain't no shit like that, but them nigga said they saw the nigga Y.G. getting out a undercover car."

"You already know what that mean—rock-a-bye-baby," Sunkist said.

"Fo sho because the nigga ain't say shit to none of us about that shit. If you got hit or picked up by the D.T.s you put that shit on the table right then, but check it, I got the nigga thinking we dropping off presents to mom Duke's and we all meeting up at D.J. Black crib to drop a CD. That will give everybody time to get to Black's crib."

"A'ight, bet that up."

"Yo, Fire good? I heard about that shit last night, but for real though you need to lay low for awhile 'cause the streets is talking, feel me?" Pressure said.

"I feel you and Fire good. She came in late night and went straight to bed. I'll see you at Black crib in a few."

Sunkist sent a couple texts for all the baby gangstas to be at 1141 South Wood Apartments A.S.A.P.

Chapter 15

Forty-five minutes had passed before Sunkist pulled up in the apartments. Damn, this shit is thick out here. Just as demanded, all the baby gangstas were there and in full effect.

Sunkist parked and got out of his car. All the homies gave their salutes and made their way inside Black's crib. B.J. and Mike were in the booth spit'n. The beat was fire and B.J. was killing it. Y.G. was the last one to pull up. He parked then him and Mia made their way inside the crib. The homie Pimp opened the door for them.

"What's up, cuz? Hey Mia," Pimp greeted them, closing the door behind them. Y.G. went through the crowd and gave everybody dap.

The beat cut and Mike and B.J. came out the booth. Pimp slid in front of the front door while Crimz blocked the back door. Y.G. didn't even notice, but Mia did. Everybody backed up against the walls of apartment, leaving Y.G. and Mia standing in the middle of the room. Y.G. looked puzzled.

"Look y'all, I don't know what is going on but I ain't got shit to do with nothing," Mia said while placing her hands in the air.

"What the fuck is going on?" Y.G. looked around the room.

Sunkist went to the kitchen and got two chairs, one for Mia and one for Y.G. He brought the chairs into the room then placed them behind Mia and Y.G. "Sit the fuck down," Sunkist spit.

Mia dropped like a sack of potatoes. She was in full compliance. Y.G. slid down in the chair watching everybody in the room.

"Now, Boo, you said you saw this nigga and the nigga was getting out of an undercover police car downtown in front of the courthouse. You got something you want to tell me, nigga?" Sunkist said while pulling his XD-40 from his waistline.

"Sunkist, let me explain, homie. I got stopped by a D.T. but I ain't tell them shit. They let me go downtown." Y.G.'s heart was pumping now. His life was in the balance.

"What they stop you for?"

"You remember the nigga Moe I robbed? That nigga told and they wanted to see if they could catch me with the gun on me, cuz. Sunkist, you know me, cuz. You know I would never flip on the crew. Look how much work I done put in for the set. I have shed blood, sweat, and tears for this shit."

Sunkist looked at Pressure. "I'm saying, cuz, the nigga do got a point and I will never take a outsider word over my homies, so this is how this gonna go…." Before Sunkist could finish his sentence Pressure held up his hand.

Something dawned on him. "If this nigga is a rat they could be listening. Where is this nigga phone at?"

"Look! Boo, I feel you on what you saying, but that's our homie, so we got to take his word. If he said that's what happen, then that's what happen."

Pressure walked over to where Y.G. was sitting and held out his hand. Everything love. Y.G. gripped his hand. Pressure punched him in his temple, knocking him out cold. Pressure held his finger to his lips motioning for everyone to remain quiet. He quickly reached in Y.G.s pocket and got his phone.

The phone was locked so he couldn't gain access. He thought for a second and looked at Mia. Every bitch knows their nigga's passcode, they just be waiting on a nigga to slip so they can catch their ass red-handed. Pressure handed the phone to Mia who quickly unlocked it and handed it back to Pressure.

Pressure went straight to his audio recorder. There were no files to be pulled up. His media player was next. He tapped on the media player and one file popped up. He tapped on the file and a video came up. He tapped play and the video started. What he saw fucked him up and he passed the phone to Sunkist so he could watch the shit.

This nigga is a certified rat. Sunkist went to his contacts and went down the list. His finger stopped on Stanburg. "Son of a bitch. Wake that bitch-ass nigga up."

Sunkist pulled out his cell to call Lil Don. Lil Don answered on the third ring. "What's good, homie?"

"Yo, we got a problem. We found out there was a rat in the organization. The nigga recorded you and Killa making that transaction. In the video you can't see your face but he got the car so get out of that car now because they probably on it. We 'bout to take care of this nigga now."

"Thanks for the heads up, homie. Peace!"

Sunkist ended the call. Y.G. was wide awake, sitting holding his head. "Come here, Mia." She got up and went to Sunkist like a small child not knowing what to expect. "Get on your knees and salute a real gangsta."

She got on her knees and unbuckled Sunkist's pants. She slid his dick out and began sucking his dick. Sunkist rubbed his pistol along the side of her face. "That's it, baby. Now, tell me how a real gangsta taste."

"You taste delicious," she spoke briefly before sliding his dick back in her mouth.

Y.G. wanted to kill Sunkist for the disrespect he displayed but there wasn't shit he could do about it.

"Now, Mia, since you have been a good girl there is a way out of this situation for you."

Mia began to suck harder hearing the good news. "You can kill and live or die with the nigga, your choice."

Sunkist slid his dick out her mouth and handed her the XD-40. "Make a choice," Sunkist said and waited for her decision. She took the gun and stared at it for a minute. Y.G. began to shake remembering she had just gone through his phone and seen the pussy pictures her friend Nikki sent him. At that moment he could see the hurt in her eyes.

"Baby, please don't do this shit. If they want to kill me let them do it."

"Shut the fuck up. Just shut…the…fuck…up. All the shit you put me through and you fucking my so-called homegirl. Nigga, please!" She lifted the gun and aimed it to his chest.

"Baby, noooo!" Boom! Boom! Boom! The shots echoed through the apartment walls.

Y.G.s body fell to the ground. He was dead but for some reason his foot was still kicking. Everyone in the apartment took out their straps and unloaded the clips into Y.G.'s body, cutting that leg off.

"Yo Grave-yard, do what you do best, find him a resting spot for the pieces that is left of him." Sunkist paid D.J. Black for his services. He put his arm around Mia's neck. "Welcome to the team." They made their way out the door but before leaving he told Pressure to get Stanburg's number out the phone then destroy it.

CHAPTER 16

Zionna touched down at Fayetteville International Airport at 11:45 a.m. She stepped off the airplane and took in her surroundings. I'm home. She took in a deep breath, smelling the air's pine trees. She exhaled. She straightened her Dolce & Gabbana shades and stepped off the plane into the terminal.

She sported a Versace suit with matching Versace boots and belt. On her wrist the ice dripped from a $122,500 Tiffany & Co. diamond watch. Cartier earrings hung from her ears.

Her phone rang. She answered without looking who was calling because if you had her number it was meant for you to have it. Speak!

"I'm outside waiting on you," Amanda Koontz said.

"I'm on my way. What car are you in?"

"A white 911 Porsche."

"Be there in a sec."

Zionna ended the call and made her way through the airport. As soon as she was out the doors, she spotted the Porsche. Koontz pulled up to the curb. She opened the door and got in.

"Did you get the information I requested?"

Koontz handed a brown folder to her. The addresses, phone numbers, and names of their closest relatives are in there.

Koontz pulled off. Zionna opened the folder. Ms. Mya Davis, aka Star, 2823 Pinewood Rd., mother's name Ruth Davis, SSN 237-72-5582, phone 910-685-2312. She flipped through the others. Shay, Meme, Nikki, and Mia. She took out Mia's file and handed it back to Amanda. "She is family now but these others, oh God, they gonna wish they never put their hands on my sister."

Koontz took a left on Owen Drive. "What's been going on recently, and please tell me some shit I don't know."

"Well, my sister has been trying to find out who William Grey's plug is so we can hit his ass for the money and the work, but we can't get a lead on shit. Speaking of your sister, I heard she is a lieutenant now, Ms. Lieutenant Ashley Lopez. Sounds sweet."

Zionna pulled out her cell to call her sister. After a couple rings Fire picked up without looking at the number. "Who the hell is dis? It's 11:55 in the morning, like what the fuck?"

"Salute a gangsta when you see a gangsta."

"O.M.G., are you here already?"

"Yes, I'm about to get a car from my car lot down here and I'll be over in a sec."

"Okay sis, see you when you get here. Love you."

"Love."

Zionna ended the call. "You got the hammer I asked for?" Koontz handed her a silver-plated Desert Eagle 45 in a plastic bag. Zionna took the pistol out of the bag. She popped the clip in and cocked the hammer back. "That's what I'm talking 'bout." She put the gun in her Chanel bag. "Take me to the lot so I can pick up a whip."

They made their way to 5 Points Auto Sales located on Bragg Boulevard. "After I speak with Sunkist I will let you know our next move. I may have someone that will lead us to paradise."

Zionna looked at her manicured nails. "I want you to find out where Stanburg rests his head at, and I want you to keep an eye on your sister to make sure her loyalty is with us and not playing both sides of the fence. We are going to eliminate our opposition starting with Sgt. Toney Jones. He works under Stanburg, correct?"

"Yes, he does." Gina McBryant, Paul Williams, Stacy Fisher, and Richard Layman are under his command. I know they are the ones that distribute the drugs after Sgt. Jones picks it up. The money is collected and given to Stanburg. Stanburg meets William Grey and gives him the money. After Stanburg gets the money, he meets with his connect, which we don't know who the connect is. For some reason they don't trust my sister because they won't pull her in. I guess she wasn't recommended by one of their own."

"Okay, since we know their operation, we got the upper hand. We will start with one of Stanburg's guinea pigs. Believe me, every pig squeals."

Zionna placed the folder under her arm. "You handle Stanburg and I'll handle Sgt. Toney Jones, starting with officer Richard Layman. Text me his address once you have it." Zionna exited the car, closing the car door behind her as she made her way toward the office building.

As she walked, she noticed a Ford Explorer to her left. Damn, that shit is ugly as fuck. What the hell is K-Ron doing? She thought. She had left Jungle and K-Ron in charge to manage the car lot. She noticed a bright 2020 Ford Mustang Shelby GT sitting on some chrome 20-inch rims.

She forgot all about K-Ron and Jungle. She ran inside and snatched the keys off the wall. Jungle spoke but it fell on deaf ears as she made her way out the door. She hit the alarm and unlocked the doors. She hopped inside and adjusted her seat. The seat was hot due to the sun, but she ignored it.

She took in the new smell of the car, and it calmed her. She hit the push to start, and the car came alive. She hit the gas a couple of times, loving the sound from the dual exhaust. The motor rocked the car slightly. She smiled as she rubbed the steering wheel like she was taming a beast.

Zi took out her cell and Bluetoothed it to the car. After they were paired, she opened her iHeart Radio app and her favorite song by Young Jeezy: "I used to have nothing, but now I got a whole lot of everything."

She fixed her shades and looked in the rearview mirror. Yeah, I'm a bad bitch. She pulled up to the entrance to the car lot, looked both ways, and hit the gas, burning rubber as she left. Ha-ha, motherfuckers, I'm back.

Chapter 17

William Grey waited patiently. He checked his watch again—3:35! *What the fuck is Peterson doing? He's been waiting for two hours to hear from him.* He tapped on the side of the window and exhaled. He glanced down at his Bulgari watch—3:40. He took out his cell to call Stanburg.

"Hello."

"Things are in motion, are you in place?" Grey asked.

"I'm down at the docks now. I'm with Sgt. Jones now and the rest of the team is on standby."

"That's good, okay! Let me call you back. The plug is calling me now." Grey quickly ended their conversation and switched calls.

"Hello! I've been waiting on your call. I have everything in place."

"Dock 313," Peterson said, and ended the call.

Grey called Stanburg back. He picked up immediately. "Yes, Mr. Grey?"

"Dock 313."

"I will take care of the rest," Stanburg said before ending the call.

Stanburg was a German soldier before he came to American soil, so he was used to following orders. He got out of the black Crown Vic. Standing six-feet-two-inches, he wiped his hand across his bald head, giving the signal for the other officers to pull up to where he was at. He stood in the middle of the old shipyard.

Three black on black Dodge Chargers pulled up coming from different directions. They parked in a circle around Stanburg. The officer was dressed in complete uniform just in case anything went sideways. This would be an undercover sting under the black ops operation.

Sgt. Toney Jones, Gina McBryant, Paul Williams, Stacey Fisher, and Richard Layman stood around Captain Stanburg waiting for their orders.

"We have 20 minutes to empty this container and be out." Stanburg set his timer on his watch. "Let's get to work." Stanburg made his way to dock 313. He reached under the front of the container and retrieved a key to the lock. He unlocked the container and opened the doors. He motioned for the officers to back their vehicles up to the container. They popped their trunks and exited their cars. Within 20 minutes they had the bricks of cocaine loaded up and ready to go.

Sgt. Toney Jones shook Stanburg's hand while the rest of the officers patted him on the back as they left, thanking him for their paid advance. "I'll be in touch," Sgt. Jones said before he left. Stanburg pulled out his cell to call Grey.

"I take it everything has been handled."

"Yes, boss, but I got to go pick my daughter up from school, so I'll be in touch."

"Good day to you," Grey said.

"To you as well," Stanburg said before ending the call.

He looked at his watch which read 4:10. Damn, I'm gonna be late. He tried to call his wife Tiffany, but she didn't pick up. He thought for a second. Lieutenant Lopez stayed in Hollywood

Heights which was right around the corner from the school. He decided to call Lopez. She picked up on the second ring.

"Hello."

"Hello, Miss Lopez, how are you?"

"I'm good, cap, how are you?"

"All in a day's work, but can you do me a favor since I'm running low on time?"

"What is it? I'm 'bout to go on break in five minutes."

"Well, since my and your daughter play on the same soccer team, I knew she wouldn't mind you picking her up. She is standing out front of Jack Britt as we speak. Can you please pick her up and drop her off at my house? Do you have something to write with?"

"Hold on a sec…okay, go 'head."

"The address is 7549 Timberland Drive, and thank you, Lopez."

"No problem, cap." Lopez ended the call.

Mia pulled up to Cape Fear Hospital after receiving a call from Star and Nikki saying they needed a ride. Mia parked and waited for them to exit the hospital. She turned her radio up and hit high on the air conditioner. She was feeling herself inside her new Toyota Corolla S Sport, complimentary of Sunkist.

Mia, born Masha Brown, was a natural born beauty. She was five-feet-five inches tall with light brown eyes. She had a Lisa Ray body with small feet, size six. Even though she had beautiful hair, she loved to rock wigs. She be on her Nikki Minaj shit. She would put you in the mind of ESPN sports reporter Maria Taylor. She sported a Vince Camuto sequined shift minidress, a pair of red Regal buckle sandals, and a Nina Breena red clutch to match. Her hair was in an up-do with red highlights that faded to orange on the tip of her hair. She wore a Rolex Date just 41 on her wrist, complimentary of Fire and Pressure. Her earrings were Basso.

She pulled out her phone and started playing Candy Crush. Twenty minutes had passed and their asses were still in there. I'm 'bout to leave their ass, she thought. She received a text. She reviewed the message: "When you get them bitches in the car come to 1623 Pine Crest Road."

Mia texted the number back: "Who the fuck is this?" She waited. A red Mustang pulled in behind her. Mia looked in her rearview mirror. She received another text: "Seven the hard way."

She knew this code came from her organization. She texted back: "Say no more."

She looked up and saw Star and Nikki coming out the exit door. Mia beeped her horn to get their attention. They made their way over to the car. Star got in the front passenger side and Nikki got in the back. Mia didn't want to be disrespectful, but goddamn Fire fucked her up. Nikki had staples holding her face together. She was holding her stomach when she got into the car.

Star had stitches across her forehead. Mia didn't want to stare, so she spoke first. "What's up, Star?" "How you feeling, Nikki?" Star was looking at her with a strange look on her face.

"I'm doing okay, but damn, you came up in the world. Just the other day you was pushing that little beat up Honda," Star said.

"I can't lie though, this shit is fly. What nigga done let you whip their shit."

Nikki said, "Oh, my bad, we heard about Y.G. Do they still got a missing person out on him?"

"Yeah, his mom is really fucked up over that shit. I'm holding up thought," Mia said.

Star took a closer look at her watch. "Is that a Rolex?"

Nikki jumped over the seat to get a better view. "Damn, bitch, put us on," Nikki said.

Star gave Mia the once over. Basso earrings, Rolex, and a new whip. This bitch came up overnight. Hair done, nails done, and everything new. Star was patiently waiting for Mia to give them the info.

"Okay, look. Y.G. wasn't my main nigga. Now that he is… well, wherever he is, I can finally do me. My nigga is paid. I was on my way to meet up with him and his friends when y'all called."

"He got friends? Shit, put us on and introduce us," Nikki said.

Star ruined the plan. "Nikki, look at us. Do it look like we need to be up in a nigga face? Bitch, have you looked in the mirror lately?" Star screamed.

"Easy, y'all. Whenever y'all get y'all selves together I got y'all, no rush, but I'm not gonna lie, this is his whip. I got to drop it off so I can get my little beat up Honda back." As Mia talked, she was putting in the location to the address she received from her organization. Once the route was in the GPS, she put her Bluetooth in her ear and pulled off.

The drive was quiet. Star was thinking about her daughter and A.p.'s mom. Nikki was thinking about how she would play these niggas out their money once she met them. Mia was deep in thought thinking about how shit was gonna play out once she pulled up to the address. She looked in her driver side mirror and saw the red Mustang a few cars back.

CHAPTER 18

Shut the fuck up, nigga, and do what the fuck I said or I'ma put your brain all over this pizza box." The skinny white boy was so scared he could barely move. Killa had snatched him out of his car. Now he had a Glock nine pressed to the side of his head. Killa had received info to where Meme and Shay lived and had strict orders to bring them to 1623 Pine Crest Road immediately.

Killa grabbed the dude by the collar and escorted him up the sidewalk. Once they were in the driveway, they made their way to the front door. Killa rang the doorbell and stepped out of view. A few seconds had passed before the door opened. "I'm sorry, but we didn't order…." Killa slapped the older woman upside the head with the pistol, knocking her out cold. All you could hear was her body hitting the ground.

The white boy looked down at the lady but before he could look up, he caught the same treatment. He laid out cold beside the old woman. Killa stepped over their bodies and made his way inside the house.

No one was in the living room. Killa heard female voices and music being played upstairs. He crept up the steps. Once he was at the top he peaked around the corner and saw Meme dancing in front of a mirror. She was dressed in her panties and bra. Shay was laid back on the bed talking on her phone.

He made his way down the hall, stopping at the side of the room's door. He peaked in again. Shay was getting up and was about to leave the room, but she stopped. "Where the hell is my phone charger?"

Killa quickly ran in the room and put the gun to Shay's head. "Bitch, if you scream, I promise you will have a closed casket."

Meme stopped dancing and thought her eyes were playing tricks on her as she looked in the mirror. She slowly turned around to face a nightmare. "We ain't got no money," Shay cried.

"Bitch, just shut the fuck up. Where is your car keys at?" Shay pointed to the dresser. "Meme, grab them keys, we 'bout to go for a little ride." Meme grabbed the car keys and they made their way out the door.

A neighbor was just coming home when they exited the house. Killa pulled his flag over his mouth and nose. Shay got in the car first on the passenger side. "Hey. Hey, what do you think you are doing?" The neighbor was coming towards Killa.

Killa lifted the Glock nine and let off two shots in his direction. He screamed like a little bitch. He had a change of heart and ran as quick as he could to get out of Dodge.

"Get the fuck in and drive," Killa demanded. Meme got in the driver's seat while Killa slid in the back. They pulled out the driveway onto Hibiscus Street. Killa told her to keep straight and make a left at the stop sign. She followed his directions until he told her to stop. "Get the fuck out and get in that Toyota RAV4 over there, the blue one." They exited the car. Killa got behind the wheel and pulled off, going to get rid of the vehicle.

The doors to the SUV opened. Souljah and Deadly stepped out looking like Mad Max and Biggs off of Shottas. "Let's go," Deadly said, holding a long barrel 44 Smith and Wesson. He was wishing one of these bitches would try something. They got in the SUV. Deadly and Souljah got in behind them.

Trearina put the car in drive and pulled off. Twenty-five minutes later she was pulling onto Pine Crest Drive. She looked in her side mirror and saw a Toyota Corolla pull in behind her followed by a red Mustang. She just kept her head straight and played it cool. She took the Bluetooth out of her ear.

She was coming up on a dead end, but she saw Fire and Pressure sitting on the hood of their cars. Grave-yard, Pimp, Mike, and B.J. were posted up. The new members to the team were standing in the driveway. Boo, Crimz, and Tee-Tee were ready to show what they were about and to put on for the organization.

CHAPTER 19

⊷o⟨⤳⟩o⊶

Trearina parked and cut the engine. Deadly and Souljah stepped out and motioned for the girls to exit. Shay and Meme got out and stood there. Star thought her eyes were playing tricks on her so she blinked and refocused.

"Bitch, I know you didn't set us up like this." Star was livid and her blood pressure shot through the roof. All she could think about was this disloyal-ass hoe. Fuck that! She punched Mia in the face as hard as she could. Mia slammed on the brakes. Zionna zipped by, slamming on brakes, whipping the Mustang in front of Mia.

She jumped out, leaving her door open. She ran to the passenger side and snatched Star completely out of the car by her hair. Nikki grabbed Mia by her hair and started punching her in the head until the back door opened, and Fire snatched her out the car by her hair. Mia jumped out the car.

"Bitch! Don't ever put your fucking hands on me," Mia screamed. Fire let Nikki go and slowly backed up. Mia was standing there shaking and crying, holding on to a pink-handled 380.

"Mia, just chill, baby girl. We just gonna have fun with these hoes. We gonna let the homies run a train on them and then we gonna let them go."

"Shut the fuck up, Fire," Mia spit.

Oh, this bitch got to be mental health talking to me like that, but she ain't mentally stable, so she got that one, plus this crazy bitch got a gun.

"A'ight, player. It's your world," Fire said, throwing her hands up.

Mia turned her attention back to Nikki. "Bitch, put that gun down and I'll beat your ass," Nikki said with eyes of hatred.

"Oh, word! How about you beat this?" Boom! Boom! Boom!

Mia walked up on Nikki and emptied the clip, watching her body jerk every time she hit her. Shay pissed on herself and Meme hit the ground. Fire slowly walked over and slid the gun out of her hand. Fire threw the pistol to Zionna. She caught it.

"Bitch, get your goofy ass up, sitting on the ground looking extra stupid. What? You ain't got that Energizer bunny shit in you no more?"

Star slowly stood up, not knowing what to expect. "What the fuck you looking at? Walk, bitch!" Star went and stood beside Meme and Shay.

"Now for the main event. Ladies, I want y'all to show y'all southern hospitality to the newest members of my organization. Gentlemen, enjoy. Yo Grave-yard, you and B.J. clean this shit up. Pressure, once the fun is over you know what to do." Pressure nodded. "Sis, come take a ride with me."

Fire and Zi walked up the street and got in Zionna's Mustang. Zionna pulled off. "I got a task for you. This life ain't forever, we live, we die, but as we live this life we live it with insurance. No one know what we speak of, not even Sunkist." Zionna handed Fire a piece of paper with the information.

CHAPTER 20

Alisha Martinez had been following Crimz all day. She had placed a tracker on his car. It didn't take her long to find out where he was and who he ran with. You would be amazed what a nigga will tell with just the thought that he might get some pussy from her. God, these niggaz are so weak.

After spinning the block a couple times and hitting a club or two, she knew where to find him and his little team, Tee-Tee and Boo.

Now she was in a vacant house across from where the tracker led her. She picked up her binoculars to get a better look at the people across the street. Someone sat on a car. She took out a notebook from her bag. She picked up her camera and adjusted the lens. First, she took a picture of the brown skinned guy. Then she snapped a couple of shots of a group of men posted up on the corner. "What the fuck?" She zoomed the camera in to make sure she saw her correctly. What is Fire doing here? She moved along to the group of guys that stood in the driveway. She took a couple of pictures, making sure to capture Crimz. She was about to take another picture, but a SUV pulled up. Then she saw two more vehicles pull up. She took more pictures of all three vehicles.

"Oh shit!" She put down her camera and picked up her binoculars to get a better look at what was transpiring. Okay, looks like a simple fight. "What are you doing, Fire?" she questioned. She looked on in excitement, wondering what was gonna happen next. A girl got out the car with a gun. What is she about to do? Boom! Boom! Boom!

She dropped her binoculars. She held her mouth for a moment. "Oh my God, she just killed that girl." Martinez grabbed her radio and called it in. "I have shots fired, victim is down, Pine Crest Drive. Repeat, I have shots fired, victim is down, Pine Crest Drive."

Martinez picked up her camera and quickly adjusted her lens. She took four more pictures of the suspects. "We copy, units are on their way." Martinez grabbed her radio, "10-4." She took out her cell and called William Grey. Grey picked up on the second ring.

"Ms. Martinez, how are you? I've been getting some good reports about you."

"Thanks, chief, but I believe I have the criminals you've been looking for. I have taken pictures of them together and one of them just committed a murder right in front of me. I have called it in and am waiting on the units now."

"Good job, Martinez. I want you to stay low and by no means show your face. I want you deep undercover. One murder is not going to put their organization behind bars for good. One will take the fall to free the rest. We got to hit them where it hurts. We got to catch them with guns, money, and drugs. Then I can hit them with criminal enterprise and bury their asses. You keep doing what you're doing and be careful with that evidence. I'm heading out to the crime scene now. Keep me informed."

"I will, sir." Martinez ended the call. She picked up her binoculars and got back to work.

CHAPTER 21

Lieutenant Ashley Lopez pulled up to Jack Britt Middle School just on time. She pulled into the parking lot and scanned the area looking for Stanburg's daughter. She had only seen her one time and that was in a picture that was taken at one of their soccer championship games. There was a group of girls laughing and enjoying themselves over by the entrance to the school. She called out the name Lilly and all the girls stopped their activities and looked in her direction, then back at Lilly. Bingo!

"Lilly, come on, your father asked me to pick you up."

Lilly said her goodbyes to her friends. "Hey, Ms. Lopez."

"Hey, Lilly, but how do you know my name?"

"Your daughter talks about you all the time."

Lopez smiled. She had two beautiful daughters. One was 13 and the other 29. "Okay, get in so I can get you home." They got in and Lopez pulled off.

Within 10 minutes Lopez was pulling into the driveway of 7549 Timberland Drive. Lopez beeped her horn before letting

Lilly out. She wanted to make sure she got in safely. Lopez saw the door to the house open and a middle-aged white woman stepped out of the house onto the porch. Lopez unlocked the doors and let Lilly out.

"Thank you, Ms. Lopez," Lilly said before opening the car door.

"You are welcome, baby."

Lilly shut the door and went to her mother, Tiffany. Lopez waved and backed out of the driveway. "Alexa, call Stanburg."

He picked up immediately. "Hello!"

"I just dropped your daughter off at home."

"Thank you, Ms. Lopez, and if there is anything that I can do for you, just give me a call."

"I will." Lopez ended the call. "Alexa, call Koontz."

She picked up on the third ring. "'Bout time you called me."

"Sorry, sis, I have been mad busy. They got me working my ass off at the station and now I'm pulling baby duties. Stanburg calls me and ask me to pick up his daughter and drop her off, so now I'm headed back to the station. I didn't even get to enjoy my break."

"My week has been crazy too. My caseload is full. I got two trials coming up next week and Grey got to be fucking the magistrate because the probable cause for a warrant is bullshit, but that's why my caseload is so full."

"I feel you, sis. How are my nieces doing?"

"They doing…well, shit! I really don't know. I mean, they always with their father. How is Mylasha and Ms. My-Shit-Don't-Stank?"

"My daughters are fine, silly! Mylasha is actually with her father and Ms. My-Shit-Don't-Stank is out in the field training to become an agent."

"Oh, that's good to hear. Who is her field trainer?" Koontz asked.

"I think it's Stacey Fisher."

"Yeah, I know him, he works with Gina McBryant and Paul Williams. They all work under Sgt. Toney Jones, and you know they all work under Stanburg."

"I see you are very in tune," Lopez said.

"What you think, I'm the head district attorney?" Both women laughed.

"Whatever, girl. I'm pulling up to the station now so I'll talk to you later."

"Okay, love you."

"Love you too." Lopez ended the call just as her radio came on.

"Shots fired! Victim down! Pine Crest Drive!"

She threw on her lights and headed to Pine Crest Drive.

CHAPTER 22

Pressure was rolling a blunt of blueberry Kush. After the blunt was rolled he lit it and took a couple of puffs. He held the smoke in his lungs for about 20 seconds and then exhaled. He laid back against the window and tuned into the orgy being performed in front of him. Star was on her knees sucking Boo's dick while Crimz was hitting her from the back. Meme was pressed up against the side of Crimz's car. Tee-Tee was slow stroking her from the back, her hair wrapped in his hands, pulling it every time he penetrated her. The bitch was looking like she was enjoying the shit. Pressure just shook his head.

Shay was laid back on top of Lil Mike's car. B.J. was standing on the hood of the car. He was leaned over the roof of the car jamming his dick in her mouth. Grave-yard was standing on the truck. Shay had her legs wrapped around his head while he ate her pussy. Mia was zoned out in her own world.

Pressure could hear sirens in the distance. He leaned up. The sirens got closer. "Yo, y'all tighten the fuck up," Pressure screamed. Niggaz was pulling up their pants and hopping off of the car. The sirens got closer. Everybody pulled out their straps.

This was a dead-end street, so if they were coming for them there wasn't but two ways out of this—carried by six or judged by 12.

The first police car turned onto Pine Crest Drive, and everybody knew they were coming for them. Pressure got behind his car and dropped to the ground. The rest also took cover. Cops were coming from everywhere. They blocked off the whole street.

Mia was standing in the middle of the street, zoned out. Her Corolla was a few feet in front of her. Police had taken their positions. "Get your fucking hands up…now!" Officer James Miller had a dead lock on Mia.

Mia followed the officer's orders and placed her hands in the air. "Officer, my baby is in my car…I got to get my baby." Mia took slow steps towards her car.

"You stop right there. One more step and I will take you down."

"I got to get my baby." Mia was at the driver's door now. She quickly ducked down. The officer couldn't get the shot off. Mia reached under the driver's seat and pulled out a subcompact XDS-45. She reached in the back seat and got her daughter's favorite blanket. She fixed the blanket in her arms to look like a baby was in the blanket. She put the gun under the blanket. She stood up.

"See, all I wanted was my baby."

Officer Miller exhaled. "Cover me, I'm going to get the baby." Officer Miller stood up from his position. "Okay now…let me see the kid."

Mia stopped in her tracks. "Y'all want to see my baby?" Mia dropped the blanket, and every officer watched the blanket drop to the ground, thinking Mia dropped her baby. It gave Mia just enough time to lift her weapon. Boom! Boom! Boom!

The first bullet caught Officer Miller right between the eyes. The second bullet hit the officer that was covering for Miller in the shoulder. The impact knocked the officer off his feet. Once Mia let off her first three shots she turned to run back to her car for shelter. The police opened fire.

Mia caught one bullet in her left leg and another in her back. She made it back to the driver's side door. She slid her body to the front of the car. Mia peaked over the hood of the car and seen several officers closing in on her. She felt the pain in her leg and knew she was hit. She felt her stomach and blood was running through her shirt. "Fuck!" she yelled out.

Pressure looked around the corner of his car. He saw Mia had been hit and the officers were closing in on her. Pressure put the pistol to his forehead and exhaled. Seven the hard way. He gripped the pistol and came up bustin'. Boom! Boom! Boom!

Grave-yard and Mike let their guns go. Deadly opened the trunk to the SUV and pulled out three AR-15s. He passed one to Souljah and threw one to Pressure. Pressure jumped behind the SUV.

Police took cover. Mia wanted to run back to her crew, but she couldn't run. She was stuck between enemy lines. Police opened fire again. Boo, Crimz, and Tee-Tee let their guns bust, keeping the cops at bay.

A Channel 11 news helicopter had arrived. Lopez pulled up to the scene. She parked and got out. Two more vehicles pulled in and parked. William Grey stepped out of one vehicle and Sgt. Toney Jones and Captain Stanburg stepped out of the other one.

The gunfire had stopped. Pressure pulled out his cell to call Sunkist, but his screen was cracked. William Grey held up his hand, motioning to the officers to stand down. Officer Jessie Clark handed Grey a loudspeaker.

"This is the chief of Fayetteville Police Department. Mr. William Grey speaking. Come out with…." Before he could finish his sentence, Pressure, Deadly, and Souljah stepped from behind the SUV and opened fire. Grey dropped the loudspeaker and took cover.

The whole crew opened fire. Bullets hit the police cars, shattering windows and flattening tires. Officer Lisa Lopante got struck in the neck and was slowly bleeding out. Ella Pitaque was trying to keep pressure on it, but it wasn't looking good. Officer Sarah Steverson had been hit in the shoulder and was laying up against her patrol car. "We need a medic now!" Ella yelled. Bullets were flying over their heads.

William Grey pulled out his cell and called to get the assistance of S.W.A.T.

Mia began to cough up blood. If she didn't get to a hospital soon she wasn't gonna make it. The gunfire had stopped. Pressure looked at Mia. She was shaking back and forth. His clip was empty. He looked around. Everybody's clip was empty. "Fuck! Fuck! Fuuuuuck!" he yelled.

S.W.A.T. was pulling in. They jumped out and took their position. They waited on orders from the chief of police. Grey walked over and picked the loudspeaker up and dusted it off.

"So, let's try this again. By now y'all should be out of bullets. There is nowhere to run. Throw y'all guns in the middle of the street and come out with your hands up. I will give y'all two minutes, then I'ma send S.W.A.T. in."

Pressure knew it was over. He would be lame to have his homies follow him into battle knowing their lives would be taken with no chance of escape. If there was a small chance of them coming out of this shit alive, he would take his chances, but there was none. Plus, Mia was dying.

Pressure threw the AR-15 in the middle of the street and came out with his hands up. William Grey smiled. Mia threw her gun and the rest followed. Star, Meme, and Shay ran to the police, telling them about the sexual assault that happened. The officer placed them in handcuffs one by one. The forensic crime van pulled up along with an ambulance.

Officer Paul Williams and Officer Gina McBryant gathered the guns out of the street and handed them over to Lieutenant Lopez. Pressure was about to be put in a police car when Captain Stanburg stepped up.

"Officer Fisher, this one I will take in personally." Stanburg escorted Pressure to his car and put him in the back.

EMS and other officers removed James Miller and Nikki's bodies. William Grey shook Stanburg's hand. He thanked everyone for performing their duties. He thanked S.W.A.T. for their assistance and waved at the Channel 11 news helicopter. Today was a good day.

CHAPTER 23

Martinez packed all of her equipment as fast as she could. Once her stuff was packed, she slid out the back. She got in her car and pulled off.

CHAPTER 24

Zionna and Fire pulled up at the crib that Fire and Sunkist shared. Sunkist was standing in the driveway talking on his phone when they pulled up. They got out of the car.

Fire could tell something was wrong. "Baby, what's up?"

"Yo, I just got off the phone with Killa and he said that the police ran up on the crew on Pine Crest."

"That's a lie, we just left them on Pine Crest." Fire pulled out her phone to call Mia.

Sunkist grabbed her hand. "What the fuck you doing?" You make that call and they gonna ping the call and come here. Matter of fact, get rid of them phones, y'all go out and get new ones. Shit is 'bout to get crazy, but this what we signed up for. Keep y'all shit tight. Don't even try to contact the homies. The feds is 'bout to be all over this shit."

Fire's phone rang. She checked the call. It was Angel. She answered it. "Yo Angel, let me hit you back 'cause I'm busy at the moment."

"Are you okay?"

"Yeah, I'm good."

"Well, call me if you need me."

"I will. Bye!" Fire hung up.

"So, what we gonna do now?" Fire asked.

"Look, I'm 'bout to be gone for about a week. I got 2.5 million in the safe. Take it and you and your sister get low until I can figure this shit out. Since Killa knows how to move and ain't on the police radar I will let him run shit while we are gone. Plus, Lil Don is familiar with him already so we can move the work through Rocky Mount and the homies out there can push to the surrounding county."

Sunkist kissed Fire and hugged Zionna. He jumped in his Alfa Romeo and pulled off.

"It's about time you come and see the Big Apple," Zionna smiled. They hopped in the whip and headed to a private air strip out in Harnett County. Zionna made a call to her man John Charles and requested her private jet. She looked over to her sister. "Bitch, you gonna love this shit."

CHAPTER 25

Detective Brad Randolph opened the door to the interrogation room and stepped inside, closing the door behind him. Grey and Stanburg were in another room looking into the interrogation room through a mirror window. No one could see them, but they could see everything.

Once the door closed, Randolph tossed the file onto the steel table. "Look, we gonna just cut through the bullshit 'cause you are not new to this and I have a 10 o'clock with a sexy little redbone. Mr. Corey Adams, if you want to see the light of day again you will cooperate with law enforcement to apprehend Mr. Joel Smith aka Sunkist. Now, if you want to play hardball, your death will be by lethal injection."

Pressure was handcuffed to a steel table. "Can I have a cigarette and something to drink?" Pressure requested.

"Give me a second," he said and left the room.

Pressure looked over at the mirror window. He knew he was being watched so he blew them a kiss.

Randolph came back in the room with a Pepsi Max soda and a single Newport. He handed Pressure the items he requested. Pressure opened the Pepsi and took a couple of sips. Refreshing! He then put the Newport in his mouth. "Can you be a gentleman and light this for me? As you can see, my hands are tied."

Randolph reached in his pants pocket and got his lighter. He lit the cigarette for Pressure and placed the lighter back in his pocket.

Pressure took a few puffs. "Okay, I will cooperate under one condition." He took a few more pulls.

"I'm listening."

"I want for…" he took a few more puffs and blew the smoke out, "I want your wife to suck this big black DICK."

Randolph smacked the cigarette out of Pressure's mouth. Pressure couldn't stop laughing.

"You son of a bitch, you think this shit is a game?" He stormed out of the interrogation room.

Pressure was still laughing when Grey and Stanburg entered the room. "Yo, y'all guys sent that bullshit in here." Stanburg walked behind Pressure while Grey held a folder up to the camera. Stanburg took out his mace and maced Pressure so he couldn't see.

"Who the fuck you think you are?" Stanburg punched him in the head. "This city belongs to us." Stanburg kicked him out of the chair. "You want to shoot at cops, motherfucker?" He kicked him in the face. Pressure remained quiet. "So, you think hard." Stanburg took out his pistol. He grabbed Pressure by his neck and pushed him back against the wall. He put his gun in Pressure's mouth. "Now, what was you saying about sucking on something?" He slid the gun out of Pressure's mouth.

Pressure spit in his face. "I said you can suck my dick." Boom! Pressure died with his eyes open. His body slid down the wall.

Stanburg placed his gun back on his hip. "Kill all reports on him, erase the warrant for his arrest. We didn't even pick him up."

Grey shook his head and they left the room. "Let this be a statement for the rest of them."

CHAPTER 26

Lopez pulled into her driveway. God, it had been a long day. All she wanted to do was eat, take a shower, and go to bed. She grabbed her purse and made her way inside her home. She was tired. She sat her purse down on the kitchen table, then washed her hands and started to prepare dinner.

"Hi mommy," Mylasha said as she made her way down the stairs. "I see you finally made it home, and dad told me to say 'hey' for him."

"I thought you was going to stay with him for awhile in the big, fancy city of California," Lopez said, changing her mind about fixing dinner for her and her oldest daughter. Now that it was gonna be three of them, "How do you feel about Pizza Hut?" she asked her daughter.

"That's cool, mom."

Lopez went over to get the phone out of her purse so she could call her daughter. She didn't pick up but sent a text saying she was busy and wouldn't be able to make their dinner date. She slid the phone across the kitchen counter in frustration. "Mylasha, can you please order the pizza for us? I'm about to take a shower."

"No problem, mom." Mylasha went to get her phone so she could order the food.

Lopez headed up the stairs to her bedroom. Once she was in her room, she began to undress, leaving a trail of clothes from the bedroom to the shower. She adjusted the water to fit her satisfaction and got in. "God, this feels so good." She let the hot water run over her body. She felt the muscles in her body loosen up. She took down her bun and let her hair fall down to her ass.

At the age of 39 she kept herself in great shape and had a body of a goddess. She ran every morning except on Sundays. She was a vegetarian and believe me, what you eat will have its effects on your body when you get older. That was her lecture to everyone.

As she relaxed, her mind traveled back in time. She was 22 and fresh out of college with a degree in criminal justice. She was volunteering at the Salvation Army on Roberson Street when her life sent her down a road she would never forget.

He was light skinned, tall, with light brown eyes. He had dreads and a swag to die for. She was hanging up clothes, watching him from afar. He was with another male that could pass to be his brother. They were looking for a table. She had stopped what she was doing to go help them out since she knew the store best.

"Excuse me," said Lopez, "but may I help you, gentlemen?"

"Nah ma, we good." They dismissed her and kept walking.

She was left there with her mouth wide open and her feelings hurt. Hold up, who the hell do they think they are? thought Lopez.

"Excuse me! I know y'all hear me talking." She was beginning to get pissed.

"Yeah, we hear, but that's not important right now, feel me?" Sunkist replied as he walked through the store, never even looking at her.

"Goddamnit! When someone is trying to help y'all black asses, at least y'all can acknowledge me."

Everyone in the store stopped what they were doing because of the outburst. Sunkist turned around. "Look ma…" he stopped speaking and they locked eyes. He licked his lips and undressed her with his eyes. She blushed and pulled her hair behind her ear. "Okay, okay, if you insist." Sunkist held up his hands.

"Thank you," Lopez said.

"Umm, what is your name?"

"My name is Lopez, but my friends call me Low. On that note, you can call me Lopez." She gave him a smirk.

"Well, Ms. Lopez, can you help find us a table? We need a extra one for the party we throwing tonight."

"Come with me."

They followed her through the store. Sunkist couldn't keep his eyes off of her. She was Hispanic, sexy as fuck, and had a fat ass. Shit! Fuck that table, what's good with her, he thought.

Finally, they got the table of their choice and Lopez got it on a discount for them. They loaded the table in their truck. Sunkist tipped Lopez for her help and got in the truck.

"Look, you should come through tonight and fuck with me."

"I don't know you like that."

"Well look, here is my number and the address to the party. Pull up if you want but it's gonna be lit."

"I will think about it."

They pulled off and she got back to work. Later on that night she hit up her sister Koontz and asked her did she want to go to the party with her 'cause she didn't want to go alone. She agreed.

They popped up at the party around 11 p.m. and it was packed. Damn, everybody and their mama was out here. They parked and made their way inside.

The house was dark and the smell of weed smoke was everywhere. She pulled out her phone to call Sunkist. He picked up but she couldn't hear anything he was saying because the music was too loud. She hung up and sent him a text message: I'm downstairs. She slid her phone back in her pocket and waited for him.

"Damn, pretty young thing, that's all you back there," the older nigga said as he palmed her ass. Lopez couldn't believe this shit. "My name is William G...."

"Nigga! I don't give a fuck what your name is. Don't ever touch me like that again." Lopez snapped on William Grey. Lopez was pointing her finger in Grey's face when Sunkist walked up.

He threw his arm around Lopez's neck. "What's good, baby? You a'ight?"

"Hell no, I ain't all right. This nigga grabbed my ass like I was his baby mama or something," Lopez said, mean mugging Grey.

"Damn, homie, now I see why you don't get no pussy," Sunkist said laughing in Grey's face.

"What, li'l nigga? Fuck you and this bitch." Just as the words left Grey's mouth Sunkist was drawing back. Sunkist let Lopez go and caught Grey square in the mouth, knocking his gold cap out of his mouth.

Once Sunkist hit Grey it was like the whole damn house jumped on Grey. They beat him out of the party and down the street. That was the last time she saw him.

The party started back like nothing ever happened. About 30 minutes had passed and gunshots rang out. Somebody shot up the party, but Sunkist made sure she was safe. Up until today her sister wouldn't even think about going to a party with her. She didn't give a fuck if it was a masquerade ball.

From that day forth they were inseparable. They were always together. She fell in love and gave him her virginity. Sunkist was deep into the streets. She wanted him home with her but the more she pleaded the deeper he got.

With her field of choice in law enforcement and Sunkist's street life, there was conflict. She had two choices. One, stay on the path she chose for herself, knowing she had a bright future. Two, she could follow behind Sunkist on a road that would lead her to jail or an early grave. She knew she had to let Sunkist go.

In the months that followed her decision she finally told Sunkist how she felt and that she was leaving him for a better her. He said nothing and walked away.

Two weeks had passed and she found out that she was pregnant. She had a choice to make, either keep the child or abortion. No matter the choice, Sunkist would never know.

The doorbell rang. The food must be here, she thought. She finished washing so she could join her daughter.

✦ 94 ✦

CHAPTER 27

Mama Maybell's house phone rang. She was in the kitchen cooking some collards, fat back, lima beans, mac and cheese, and pork chops. She turned the stove down and wiped her hands then picked up the phone.

"Oh my God, Mama-May, they found Pressure dead behind the old Dollar General on Ramsey Street."

"Baby, what did you say? You know my left ear don't work so good."

"Your son is dead, Mama-May!" Tisha yelled through the phone.

Mama-May had to hold on to the kitchen hall to keep from falling. She slowly hung up the phone. God, sometimes I get weak. I need you to cover me, oh God. Give me the strength to carry on. She headed back to the stove, turned the flames back up, and tried to finish her meal.

CHAPTER 28

The Cumberland County jailhouse was out of control. The jail was in a full-blown raid. Everyone had been watching the news and saw how everything had played out on Pine Crest. Now, bits and pieces were removed from the video footage.

Now they were showing a breaking news report of a man found shot to death behind a Dollar General store. Come to find out it was Pressure. Everybody knew the police had something to do with his death. Upon the major's request, the TVs were shut off and the jail was put on full security lockdown.

Mia was feeling a little better. She got up and came to her cell door. The pod officer told her to get ready for court. She brushed her teeth and washed her face. After her hygiene was done she pressed the intercom button to let the officer know she was ready.

The officer popped her door and to her surprise she saw Sunkist's sister Helena. She was happy to see a familiar face. Helena patted her down. "You got your I.D. on you?" Helena asked as she continued to search her.

She felt something slide in her jumpsuit pocket. "You forgot your I.D. Please go get it," Helena said.

Mia made her way back to her cell. Once she was in her cell she reached in her pocket and pulled out a small phone. It was the size of your thumb. She powered it on. Once the phone was on, she went to the contacts. Everybody's new numbers were in it. She couldn't stop smiling until her back started hurting. She slid the phone under her pillow and exited the cell.

"I got my I.D., officer."

Helena put the handcuffs on her, then shackled her. Helena announced over her radio that she had one 72 ready for court. "Sunkist told me to tell you be strong. Seven the hard way."

Thank you, Mia said and made her way out the block. Two officers were waiting for her with nasty looks in their eyes.

"You got your I.D., bitch?" officer Lotaf spat.

"Nah, but I got your mama's old panties in my pocket."

Officer Lotaf punched her in the stomach. She dropped to her knees in pain. The pain was so severe she began to cry.

"Get your little black ass up," officer Patrick yelled.

"Welcome to our world. Motherfuckers ain't got no guns in here," Lotaf yelled. Lotaf spit in her face.

"That's enough now, go ahead and take her to court," Sgt. Loporte said. She wasn't for the bullshit but understood the officers' feelings.

Mia got to her feet. She looked down the hall and saw a line of inmates coming down the hall in chains. As they got closer she began to smile. "Homie, capital Hz Mia. We love you, homie. Love you, Mia." Hz, she gave her salute.

"I love y'all too," she yelled.

The officers were pissed and wanted to fuck her up right there but knowing to disobey a directive from their superior would cost them their jobs. They just made sure she stayed separated from the others.

Once they reached booking, they were placed in holding cells. Once the cell door closed, they began to talk. "What's good, my nigga?" Boo said, embracing Crimz.

"It ain't shit, my nigga."

Tee-Tee ran up and hugged them both. He really missed his brothers in crime. B.J., Mike, and Pimp gave their salutes. Deadly and Souljah posted up at the cell door really not in the mood for convo but did acknowledge the homies.

"Yo, y'all niggaz online?" Boo questioned.

"Yeah, I am," Crimz said.

"Yeah, I got my phone yesterday," Tee-Tee announced.

"Yeah, we good too," Souljah and Deadly said. Mike, B.J., and Pimp shook their heads in agreement.

"Helena really been coming through for us," Mike said.

"Hell yeah, much respect," B.J. said.

"Man! You see that bullshit that's on the news, man? Them motherfuckers killed cuz and now they covering that shit up, cuz."

Everyone stopped talking when the cell door opened. Grave-yard stepped in and the C/O closed the door. Everybody ran up and embraced him. "Much love, homies. Damn, it feel good seeing y'all. Where they got Mia at?" Grave-yard asked.

"She next door, cuz, she good though," Crimz said.

"You good, homie?" Boo asked.

"Yeah, homie, but it's a long road ahead of us. We got to stay strong. R.I.P. almighty Pressure. We all got phones so stay in contact with each other. Remember, seven the hard way," Grave-yard said.

"Seven the hard way," everybody repeated.

"Now, let's handle our business with these government police."

Everybody posted up and waited on the transfer van so they could be escorted to the courthouse. After 30 minutes the cell door opened, and they were escorted to a van parked outside. Everybody was surprised to see Sunkist's sister Tasha at the back of the escort van. Everyone spoke to her as they got in the back. Tasha closed the back door and locked it.

Within seven minutes they were pulling into the courthouse. The driver waited for the gate to open. Once the gate was open, they pulled in and parked. Tasha got out and unlocked the back door of the van. Officer Selma stood guard and watched the in-mates one by one exit the van. Once the last detainee was out of the van, Tasha secured the door.

Officer Selma waved his key card and a side door to the court-house opened. He held the door for officer Tasha. He stood guard and officer Tasha took the lead. Officer Selma closed the courthouse door. He took the tail, watching each detainee as they walked through the tunnel under the courthouse.

The came to an elevator. Officer Tasha took out a key and opened the elevator. They all got on the elevator and went up to the upper level. Once they reached the upper level they were greeted by four other officers who took over.

"Gentlemen, y'all are over here for your first appearance. Any questions you may have, address it to your attorney." Officer Scott finished his speech and opened the holding cell. The other officers began taking the shackles off of them. Once they were in the hold-ing cell officer Scott closed the door.

The officers stood around talking until the elevator door opened and Mia stepped off. The shackles were taken off of her and she was put in the holding cell by herself.

CHAPTER 29

"Your honor, I would like to have a brief moment with you before we begin," Amanda Koontz asked.

"Approach the bench, Ms. Koontz."

"Your honor, I would like to pass these next couple of cases to my assistant district attorney Ms. Lisa Whitfield. My caseload is extremely overloaded."

"Okay, Ms. Koontz, your request is granted, but since these cases were initially assigned to you, I would like it if you would assist Ms. Whitfield with the first appearances."

"No problem, your honor, and thank you."

Assistant district attorney Whitfield shook Ms. Koontz's hand. She was new and needed the experience of a high-profile case and this was it.

"All rise, the honorable Judge Aaron price is presiding. Y'all may sit, court is in session."

Ms. Whitfield stood. "Your honor, the first case is state of North Caroline versus Tommy Smith."

Boo entered the courtroom. He was escorted to the first table.

"Mr. Tommy Smith is charged with….she flipped the page, flipped another page, and looked at Koontz. "Ummm… your honor, he is charged with shooting in occupied property, four counts of attempted murder, six counts of conspiracy to sell/deliver a schedule two substance, seven bricks of cocaine. The list goes on and on. Mr. Smith is a level six, your honor, with outstanding warrants in 13 other counties. The state is requesting no bond, your honor. Mr. Smith is a complete menace to society."

"Mr. Smith, judging by your criminal history and warrants in other counties, at this time I will agree with the state to impose no bond. Would you like to obtain a lawyer or would you like the court to appoint counsel?"

"I will hire counsel, your honor. Now, can I get back to my cell? I'm missing my afternoon yoga class."

The judge shook his head. "Have a good day, Mr. Smith."

"Next we call Miasha Brown." Ms. Whitfield took a seat. "Why you didn't tell me that these motherfuckers was plain-out crazy," Whitfield kicked Koontz under the table.

"This is what you wanted, so this is what you got," Koontz smiled.

Mia entered the courtroom. She was escorted to the first table.

"Your honor, the case before us is state of North Carolina versus Miasha Brown. She is charged with one count of shooting in an occupied property, two counts of first-degree murder. The defendant is a level... she has no record." Why would her first charges be so serious? She looked over at Mia. She had a baby face and looked nothing like a criminal. She was convinced that Mia had got mixed up with the wrong crowd. "Your honor, the state is requesting a $500,000 bond with the condition of GPS."

"Ms. Brown, I will agree with these conditions due to the severity of these charges. Would you like to hire a lawyer or have the court appoint one to represent you?"

"Court appoint, your honor."

"Your next court date is September 9 in courtroom 2B. You take care, Ms. Brown." Whitfield was completely exhausted by the time she finished with everybody. She gave Koontz a look, and boy if looks could kill, Koontz was D.O.A.

CHAPTER 30

Mount Zion Baptist Church was packed. Everybody that was somebody was in attendance. Hustlers, pimps, killers, entrepreneurs all came to see and pay their respects to the almighty Pressure.

Once the church was full, the pastor, Mr. McHall Shalton, took the floor. Eyes were on the golden casket that sat in the front of the church. "Everyone may have a seat." The crowd took their seats.

The pastor made sure everyone was seated before he continued. "We all are here today to welcome our brother Corey Adams home. We are here today to show our love and respect to a legend and a street we all came to love. In life we must live, but to enter the paradise that the lord almighty have prepared for all of us we must depart. Depart from the ones we love most. I used to take Lil Adams to the candy store when he was little to buy him candy. Ain't that right, Mama-May? That little boy wouldn't eat one piece. He would sell every piece and put the money in his pocket. We all will miss him deeply. Now, Pressure asked that if he fell in them streets that this song would play at his funeral. At this time, we will play that selection."

The sound began. "How many niggas fell victim to the streets? Rest in peace young nigga, there's a heaven for a G, be a lie if I told you that I never thought of death, my niggas, we the last ones left."

Tears began to fall as the crowd listened to 2Pac's words. Life was too short. One minute you're laughing and joking with family and friends, next minute family and friends are laying you to rest.

The song came to an end. The pastor opened the church so those who wanted to view the body could. Mama Maybell took a deep breath and collected her energy. She exhaled and made her way to her son. She got to the edge of the casket and began to shake. Pastor Shalton grabbed her arm so she could lean on him for support.

Mama Maybell had been sent money from Fire so that he would be buried in only the best. Look at my baby. My baby. Pressure was dressed in a royal blue Versace suit, a pair of black Versace shoes. He had custom cuff links with the 2-1/10 carat diamonds spelling out his name. His arms crossed his waist. He wore a two carat t.w. necklace in platinum with the letter P on the charm. His casket was solid gold with the inside dressed in midnight black.

Mama Maybell leaned over the casket and kissed her son for the last time. She made her way back to her seat thinking he always said carried by six or judged by 12.

CHAPTER 31

Fire had been in New York going on two weeks. The Big Apple was cool. She enjoyed the city life momentarily. She tried to stay busy, but this wasn't her stomping grounds. She did want to go see the Statue of Liberty. She had a dream when she was in middle school that when she got older, she was gonna travel the world. These days it was hard to cross the street. She enjoyed the time she was spending with her sister, but this shit was getting old real quick. She was becoming homesick.

She hadn't talked to Sunkist in the two weeks she was here. She only hoped he was okay. Just then she remembered the piece of paper her sister had given her in the car when they were leaving Pine Crest Drive. She opened her purse to retrieve the piece of paper. Once she got it, she went over to a park bench and sat down.

She unfolded the piece of paper and began to read:

First, I want to say I love you more than life itself. We are twins. When you hurt, I cry. When you inhale, I exhale. When I left Fayetteville and came to New York it wasn't because I wanted to, I had to. I had to let go of you so you could actually feel something in that heart of yours. I will never give myself to another. I am a killer by blood, it's in my D.N.A. I seen from the moment you met Sunkist you would fall in love. Y'all are meant for each other. I want to give you my dream since I cannot live it. This is the address to a mansion I would share with my husband-to-be. There is no geological map of this location, I made sure of it. You have a landing field with your own private jet. There is an escape tunnel. Believe me, you never know. In the face of trouble this is your safe haven. Love, Zi.

A small tear fell from the corner of her eye. She folded the piece of paper and put it back in her purse.

She made up her mind right then and there. She would put the team on her back no matter the outcome. She pulled out her phone to call her sister so she could schedule a private flight to her safe haven.

CHAPTER 32

Martinez was doing all the groundwork. She was only 18 but was a fast thinker and she was fast on her feet. With leads from her superiors, Grey and Stanburg, she was putting the pieces to the puzzle fast. She sat on the edge of her desk and stared at her bulletin board.

Sunkist was at the top. Next was Pressure with an X by his picture. She walked over to the board and removed Pressure's picture. She tossed it in the trash. Well, no need for that. She slid Fire's picture next to Sunkist.

After receiving the video from Captain Stanburg of a drug transaction she had done a couple of computer-focused analysis and captured a picture of Killa's face. She placed his picture on the board next to Deadly and Souljah. She slid Grave-yard's picture under Sunkist and Fire. There was no need to be concerned about the rest, they were just pawns in the game.

She sat back on her desk. Now, let's see, who is Sunkist's supplier, and where is he now? Wherever he is at Ms. Unique will not be too far away, she thought. She came up with nothing. Okay then, I will go after Mr. Killa. She would later call Stanburg and make sure a warrant for his arrest wasn't issued. Let him think he is in the clear and hopefully he will lead us to something good.

CHAPTER 33

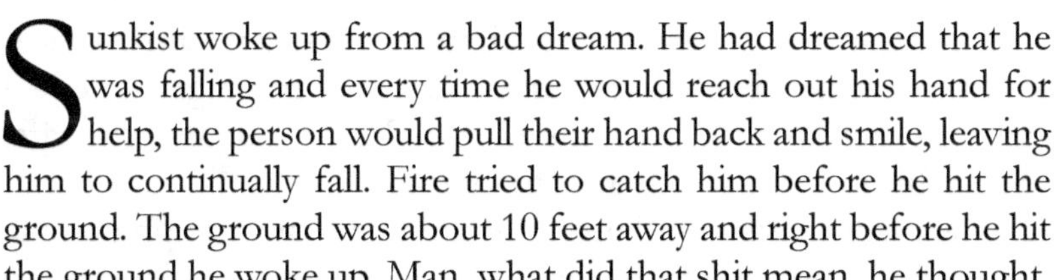

Sunkist woke up from a bad dream. He had dreamed that he was falling and every time he would reach out his hand for help, the person would pull their hand back and smile, leaving him to continually fall. Fire tried to catch him before he hit the ground. The ground was about 10 feet away and right before he hit the ground he woke up. Man, what did that shit mean, he thought.

He shook the dream off and looked around the aircraft. He was alone. He looked out the side window. He could see the beautiful Pacific Ocean. A calm feeling came over him and he finally relaxed. He was tired. This wasn't the life he wanted and it damn sure wasn't what he signed up for so many years ago.

He'd joined the organization to bring forth change. To establish communities with opportunities. To help with the racial injustice towards blacks. He wanted to show the minorities a better way to provide for themselves and their families.

For the first couple of years the movement was righteous, taking the drug money and using it to build businesses and employ members of the community. Then the objective changed once NappBasher got locked up and sentenced to life in the fed.

The team fell under Zionna's control. She was the Capital H.B.I.C. period. NappBasher ran the team from the fed. Zionna put the work in on the streets and Sunkist handled the finances and distribution. They were unstoppable. Completely untouchable. Now, with Unique by his side he'd seen a desire in her that was hidden for many years. He'd seen a desire to be free. Free completely.

He was looking at what he bought her, the life he gave her, but in all actuality, she had given him something that money could never buy and that was a woman's love. Fire gave him a desire that ran deeper than any ocean. She would give her life for him without a second thought.

Loyalty in the heart of a woman is a jewel he wore with respect and dedication. His loyalty and obligations were to the organization, but now that his perspective of the game had changed, so did his goals and opinions. In life you live for the future. Number one key to survival is self-preservation.

The plan was slowing down and preparing to land. He checked his phone to see if he had any missed calls or messages. Fire had called numerous times. He missed her already, but she was safe, and at this point that is all that mattered.

The plane landed in Manila, the capital of the Philippines. He got his bags and exited the plane. The sky's air was cool. A breeze was blowing off the Pacific Ocean. The sky had a few clouds, but the weather was nice.

As passengers passed him, he noticed they were all heading in one direction. A lot of the passengers were cadets and wore suits from the Merchant Marine Academy. They were in training for prestigious positions. Those who succeed are ensured a path to a middle-class life for their families, so they made their way to the cargo ship as quickly as possible.

Sunkist decided to grab a bite to eat as he waited on his plug. There was a line of shops that sold everything from shoes to makeup. He passed an all-women pawn shop and an Ablaza Pawnshop. Many of them offered their services. Something smelled good. He followed his nose and came across a little stand on the corner.

"The food is great here."

He jumped…not out of fear but out of unexpectedness.

John Charles smiled to himself seeing his reaction. "You okay? Do you need a hug? I see you slippin' on your pimping."

Sunkist gave his friend and mentor a brotherly hug. "Nah, I'm never slippin', just pimpin'," Sunkist shot back. Both men laughed.

"This here is called banh mi," pointing to the food Sunkist was smelling. Charles ordered two plates. He paid for the food and the men began walking.

"You have come a long way in such little time, but you have great storms, and your heart is heavy, my friend. The seconds only look to the minutes and the minutes look to the hours. Question is, who time is you really own?"

Sunkist was puzzled how he could tell his situation before he opened his mouth. This was the only man he held above himself. For one to lead, he must once follow.

"Sunkist, you are like a son to me. Yes, business has always been good, but I value our friendship over every dollar you could ever give me."

There was a park up ahead of them. They headed to the park to continue their conversation. There was a table in the middle of the park where people played chess. They took their seats at the table.

They ate in silence, enjoying their meal. When their meal was finished, Charles collected their plates and disposed of them in the trash. Once back at the table he reached in his pocket and retrieved a small black bag. He opened the bag and poured the chess pieces on the table. "What color do you want? Or you aggressive and take the initiative. If you do, I advise you on this day to choose white. Now, if you are feeling conservative and want to analyze your opponent's moves who poses a serious threat, on this day I advise you to choose black."

Sunkist thought about Grey. He couldn't attack the chief of police head on. He had to analyze his moves and let his counter move destroy him. To do this he would have to play the defensive role and be patient. He chose the color black.

Both men set their pieces up and began to play. Sunkist moved his king pawn up two squares. "In life every move you make is strategic. You got to know how to use your soldiers, but most importantly you have to know the position and quality of your soldier. Every soldier is not a killer."

Charles moved his king pawn up once. "I understand that, but I also understand that if the soldier's goals don't match his footsteps, he is stagnated, and the team becomes jeopardized because of a weak link." Sunkist moved his queen pawn up two squares.

"A weak link can be fixed with the right tools and understanding, but if you pedal too hard the chain will break. If you take steady strides you can make it to your destination without trouble." Charles moved his queen pawn up two squares.

"Sixty-four squares on this board. How can you stand on all of them and control every piece in the game?" Sunkist asked, moving his right castle pawn up one.

"To control the streets, you must first control the game. To control the game, you have to be above the game. Men follow two things—money and pussy. Women follow money and pain. To build you must destroy. How can you say you love if you have not sacrificed?" Charles moved his right bishop diagonal three squares.

"I have sacrificed my time, money, and life for the love of this organization." Sunkist moved his queen up one.

"You speak of yourself in the essence of love and sacrifice, but your best will never be good enough for the street you are trying to claim, so your sacrifices are in vain, and the fruits of your labor will never truly prosper."

Sunkist thought about Pressure and how he brought him into the organization. Now his homie lay six feet under. He thought about Mia and how he made her suck his dick and kill Y.G. Now she has been shot and faces the rest of her young life in prison.

"Sunkist, you can't catch a ray of sunshine, but you can enjoy the feeling, meaning you can't change the world, but you can enjoy the few precious moments that life offers." Charles moved his right castle knight.

"We work so hard to get rich, but once we have everything we want we are lost. If you was to gain the world and everything in it, what do you really have? The answer is nothing. We was born to die. This world is going to end and everything that you have work for is going to vanish. Over time, even the memory of your existence will fade."

"I feel you on that." Sunkist moved his knight.

"What do you really want in life? Because you can live a lie and be happy. You have to live in your truth to be completely happy."

Sunkist thought for a second. "I want a family with Unique. I want to share time with my sisters that I have misled as a brother. I want to live life free without complete chaos."

"If this is what you want, you have to take the necessary steps to make that happen. If people don't have your best interest at heart, they were never for you. Always remember you can change your future, but you must respect the past." Charles moved his queen. "Check."

"They say if you love your woman you wouldn't jeopardize her life," referring to Charles using his queen to check him. "Sometimes a woman sees what you can't." Sunkist moved his knight, blocking the check. "Out of check."

"Pointless moves is a waste of time. Patience. One's trash is another man's treasure. What you may think is a waste another man will kill for in that moment." Charles moved his knight into Sunkist's territory.

"The more danger you have in your surroundings, the more you will have to fight to protect what you love most." Sunkist moved his castle pawn up one to threaten his knight. "In the face of danger you show what you are made of," Sunkist said.

"A soldier never picks and chooses his battles. All men are equal, but one's pride never should stand in the way of a smart decision." Charles moved his knight in retreat.

Sunkist moved his bishop. "Check."

"The student shall never outshine his master." Charles

moved his pawn up one, blocking the check. "Out of check. Your move, grasshopper."

Sunkist smiled at the comment.

"See, in this game, sometimes your weakness can be your strength IF you use your weakness correctly. The heart is the weakness to all of man. Yes, that is an essential part of the human design. There is nothing new under the sun, just innovated ways to redo what's already been done."

Sunkist castles, moving his king to his right and placing his castle beside his king.

"Sometimes in life you have to change the course of your direction to seek your dreams."

As the words left Charles' mouth Sunkist contemplated on his last sentence. Grey knew his motive, knew his train of thought, but most of all knew his weakness, and that was the organization. Grey could never come close to catching him, but that wasn't the purpose of Grey's strategy. Grey would make it appear he was at his head but all along the streets gave him the tools to destroy himself. He thought about what 2Pac's mother told him: They are going to come after you, but they are going to give you the tools to destroy yourself.

Charles could see in Sunkist's demeanor he was in deep thought. "No one can fix your problems, only you can, but sometimes you need someone that cares enough for you to bring out what's already in you." Charles moved his knight and captured Sunkist's bishop.

Sunkist captured Charles' bishop with his pawn. "For every action there is a reaction, Mr. Charles. Question is, will you be ready for the reaction?"

Charles moved, pawn up one… or should he corner his queen? He contemplated for a second. Let me see if he has true love for the women in his life. Charles chose to corner Sunkist's queen. Charles moved his bishop to threaten his queen.

Sunkist moved his queen out of danger and prepared to cover her. Just as he thought.

"There is no I in team, Sunkist. Every piece on your team is equal. You have to know this because once it's time for a member of your team to react to a situation, you can cost them their life by confusing them in their position that you gave them." Charles moved his castle into the territory of Sunkist's queen.

Sunkist moved his queen deeper into cover. The love he had for Fire blinded him from his true mission. Just the threat caused him to react. Checkmate in four. Sunkist moved his castle behind his queen. In your dreams. Sunkist was now focused on what was important which was the game and not his queen. "God didn't put everybody here to live. Some was put here to die so others can live."

Charles made a conservative move to see what Sunkist was up to. Charles moved a pawn up one. Sunkist moved his bishop diagonal. "Check."

Charles moved over one space. Sunkist moved his knight, capturing Charles' pawn and placing him in check. Charles moved over again. Sunkist captured Charles' knight with his queen.

"I guess you was right, sacrifices has to be made for the greater good. You are right but sacrificing your queen for a knight is just a dumb decision." Charles picked up his pawn to take Sunkist's queen and noticed the position of the knight and Sunkist's castle. Charles tried to set the piece back down and move another piece.

"No, no, no! Remember, touch and move," Sunkist said.

Charles took the queen with his pawn.

"See, fast decisions lead to quick mistakes." Sunkist moved his castle and captured Charles' pawn. "Checkmate."

Charles was impressed. Even though he lost the game, he knew he had accomplished what he came to do, and that was to get Sunkist back on track and focused on what was important, separating the irrelevant.

Sunkist stood to shake his friend and mentor's hand. "Thank you, Charles."

"Anytime, friend. How about you take a day off and enjoy what the Philippines has to offer? Everything on me. Do we have a deal?"

Sunkist felt like the world had been lifted off his shoulders. "Okay! You have a deal, under one condition."

"And what might that be?"
"You buy us some more of that banh mi stuff."
Both men busted out laughing.

CHAPTER 34

Grey got home around 11:30 at night. He unlocked his door and entered his home. His house was far out in the countryside of Harnett County in a town called Benson. He loved the country and bought this house to escape the city life, most of all to get a peace of mind and collect his thoughts. He opened his door and hit the light switch, cutting on the lights in the living room. He shut the door behind him. He tossed his keys on the table and took off his suit jacket. He hung up his jacket.

Today was a long day but things were finally coming together. He went to the kitchen to get himself a beer out of the fridge. After he got his beer he stood by the sink, looking out on the country. The moonlight laid perfectly on the lake behind his house and the trees swayed along with the night wind.

He took a sip of his beer. He thought about Lopez. Even after all these years later he still wanted her. Just the smell of her did something to him. Once he found out that she was working for the police department he knew this would be the last chance he had to finally fuck her, but after she found out that he had children with her sister she never even looked in his direction again.

Once Peterson pulled him in on a favor to Stanburg he got his captain position, which ranked him over Lopez. After meeting the community's demands and being involved in the community he gained their respect and knew that it would lead him to a position of power. He was plugged in on the streets and only needed a platform in the world of the majority. He talked to Peterson about the chief of police position and Peterson made the active chief retire with benefits.

If he couldn't have Lopez by choice, then he would fuck her by force. Plus, now that he had dirt on her it would make it that much easier. Over the last few months he'd had her phone monitored. He knew she was still in love with Sunkist and he knew she would eventually call him and meet up with him, and he was gonna nail both their asses. But the calls she did make to Sunkist only lasted a couple of seconds. It wasn't enough time to get their location.

He went back in the living room and sat down on the couch. A beer had him feeling good but still didn't take the edge off. He got up and went over to his liquor cabinet. A bottle of Skyy vodka caught his attention. He opened the cabinet and pulled out the vodka. He sat the bottle down on the living room table and headed to the kitchen to get a glass and some ice. This what I'm talking about, he thought.

He returned to the living room and sat down on the couch. He picked up the bottle of Skyy vodka and poured him a cup. He sat the bottle down. "Cheers," he shouted, then began laughing. He laid back with his drink in hand. He pulled out his phone as he took his first couple of swallows. He put the cup down and stared at his phone for a second.

Once his mind was made up, he went to his contacts and called Lopez. No one answered. Fuck! He picked up his cup and drank some more. He put the cup back down. He called Lopez again.

After a few rings, she answered in a sleepy voice. "Hello?"

"I have a report we need to go over."

"It's 12:01 in the morning, can't it wait until I come in?"

"No, get your ass up and get over here. I'm texting you the address now."

"You not at the office? Hello? Hello?" I know this nigga didn't just hang up on me. Lopez ended the call.

She got up, took a quick shower, and did her hygiene. She got dressed. She went over to her nightstand and got the letter she wrote to Sunkist. She could never tell him face to face the truth, but the love she had for him he deserved to know. Too much time had passed, and he was kept in the dark. She didn't know if Sunkist would kill her or turn his back on her for her choices, but it was a fate that she was willing to face. She had the letter addressed to her sister Koontz so she could give it to Sunkist when the time was right.

She peeked in on her daughter Mylasha. She was sound asleep. She grabbed her purse and headed out the house, locking the door behind her.

She hit the alarm on her car, unlocking the doors, and got in. She cranked her car up and got her phone so she could put the address in her GPS. The drive was 40 minutes away. You've got to be kidding me. I got some words for this motherfucker when I get there. She hit the steering wheel with her hand. She put the car in drive and pulled off.

She stopped the car, almost forgetting to mail the letter to her sister for Sunkist. She put the car in reverse and backed up to the mailbox. She put the letter in the box and made her way to Benson, North Carolina.

CHAPTER 35

Club Diamond was lit. The parking lot was packed. Club Diamond was known for the baddest bitches in all the surrounding counties, especially the exotic ones.

Killa was in full groove mode. Since Sunkist and Fire left him the city, he was invincible. He was dressed in a black wife beater, Dickies black shorts, and sported a pair of black and orange LeBron sneakers. The sneakers were customized with his name written in cursive. He wore a black and orange Astro fitted with the matching belt. His Cartier chain hung down to his chest.

The chain lit up the room when he stepped in the club. He came through the side door and headed straight to V.I.P. to meet up with the rest of the homies.

Killa had the streets booming with work. Ever since he teamed up with Lil Don the work moved like water. He wanted to show Lil Don he appreciated him stepping in and holding him down when the set needed it the most. Sunkist was gone. Fire was M.I.A. and the whole team was locked up. It was cool, though. He made sure to send money for those that were locked up and paid for their lawyers.

He stepped into the V.I.P. The party had started without him. Lil Don had two strippers on him. Lil Don didn't even see him come in. One stripper sat on his lap in a reverse cowgirl position. She had her face pressed up against Lil Don's face. She had her hand in Lil Don's pants caressing his dick. Lil Don noticed Killa standing there waiting on him. Lil Don asked the females to excuse themselves. The strippers got themselves together while Lil Don adjusted his pants.

Lil Don stood to greet Killa as the strippers left the V.I.P. room. "What's good, cuz? Let me introduce you to the rest of the homies," Lil Don said. "Since we all run in the same circle, I thought we could all do great business together. This is Sumo 'Dirt Gang' from Durham. Him and Pressure knew each other well. This is Tiny Diamond. He came out to support our movement. This is Tiny Harlem and BK Red, they are also 'Dirt Gang.' They have a better pipeline to move the work. They have a tractor trailer company and will move the work from one coast to another."

Everyone gave their salutes in agreement. "Now, shit, let's get this shit cracking," Lil Don shouted.

The strippers came back in and this time they brought six more with them. Killa was accustomed to this type of shit. It didn't excite him. He had money on his mind. "Yo, enjoy y'all self, I'll be in touch."

Killer left the V.I. P. and headed to the bar to get something to drink. There was a small crowd around the bar. Once the crowd saw Killa coming they parted like the Red Sea. Only one female didn't move. She had her back to him and was ordering her drinks. Killa stood behind her.

From the back she was a dime. She was light skinned, small waisted, and damn, her ass looked so soft. She wore an all-white ASOS Red Carpet Geo embellished paneled midi-dress with cutout back. Her black hair was wrapped into a French bun.

She got her drink and turned around. "Oh, shit!" She jumped back, spilling her drinks on her dress. "Oh my God...look at my dress."

Killa bent down to pick up the broken glass. "Are you okay?" he asked her. She just stared at him. Damn! "Cat got your tongue?" Killa asked the bartender for a small trash can so he could put the broken glass in.

Killa stared back at her. She was gorgeous but looked kind of young. "Look, I'm sorry about your dress, and I know I ruin your night. Is there any way I can make it up to you?"

He don't know who I am, she thought. "Well, for starters you can pay for my dress, and second, you can give me my money back for those drinks." She stood with her hand on her hip with her other hand out waiting on him to give her the money.

"Money ain't shit, but what's your name?"

"My name is Pay Me," she smiled. Her smile is what turned him on and he knew he had to have her.

"Look, I make you a deal. Let me take you out so I can show you how I'm truly feeling about you right now, plus it will give me a chance to get to know you."

"I don't know, you look like a killer and a dope boy. What's your name?"

Killa just smiled. "Well, I guess I look like my name. My name is Killa."

"Oh, you must be the Killa everybody be talking 'bout. Listen, fuck all that, let's talk about you. My name is Candy," she lied.

"Nice to meet you, Candy." Whatever. "Do you have a number?" Killa asked.

"No, but you can give me yours." She handed Killa her phone so he could put his number in her phone. He handed the phone back to her.

"How old are you?"

"I'm old enough not to choke when shit get hard." She smirked and walked off.

He went to the bar and finally ordered his drink. Candy left a first impression that he thought about for the rest of the night.

CHAPTER 36

L opez turned down along the dirt road. "You have arrived at your destination," the GPS announced. She cut off the GPS. She kept driving until she saw the big house. She pulled up and parked. She grabbed her phone and sent Grey a text stating she had arrived. She sat in her car and waited for a response. Within 20 seconds he texted back. She checked the message: Come in the door is open.

She grabbed her purse and keys. She slid her phone in her purse and got out. She didn't even bother locking her car doors. There was nothing out here but dirt and woods. Unless a deer was going to steal her car, she didn't have anything to worry about.

The morning air was cold against her skin. Damn, I should have put on a coat. She only had on a white tee and some leggings. She wasn't expecting to be here long.

She made her way to the front door. She was going to ring the doorbell but remembered the door was open. She turned the doorknob and the door opened. She stepped in the house and closed the door behind her.

Grey was on a couch with a laptop on his lap. "Come on in and have a seat."

Lopez sat her purse down and thought she smelled alcohol. She noticed a bottle of Skyy vodka sitting on the living room table. She sat down in a chair by the couch.

"Was the drive long, Low?" He called her by her teenage nickname.

"No, the drive was only 40 motherfucking minutes! And my name is Lopez."

"I want you to keep that same energy because it's going to be a long night." The way he said it sent a chill down her spine. "Let me ask you something, Low, why wouldn't you ever give me a chance? I'm talking about a real chance to love you."

"Okay look, I see you are drunk I'm 'bout to leave 'cause you are tripping." Lopez stood to leave.

"Sit the fuck down!" Grey screamed.

"Motherfucker, you ain't my daddy." She grabbed her purse off the table and headed for the door. Boom! She could feel the wind off the bullet as it passed her ear. She stopped in her tracks. She left her gun in her car.

"I said sit the fuck down." She slowly turned around. Grey had set the laptop on the living room table. He was sitting on the edge of the couch with both feet planted firmly on the living room floor. Lopez sat back down. "When I ask you a fucking question, I want an answer," he spat.

"Okay, William G., let me tell you why. For one, you are disrespectful. Even when we was younger you didn't show me any respect. Before you even knew me you just walked up and grabbed my ass. Then you tried to make me fuck with you. Then the one chance I gave you I find out you been fucking my sister for years and have not one, but two children by her. Then you paid her not to tell me. That's my blood sister. What, you don't think she was going to tell me? Your problem is you think the sun only shines on your ass and you throw shade on everyone else. You couldn't have me, so you got my sister to throw that shit in my face."

"Okay, I will give you most of that, but you sit here and judge me like you are Miss Perfect. When you took this job, you knew your duties to law enforcement, but you chose to associate yourself with criminals."

"What the fuck is you talk? I ain't associated with no criminals."

"I now see you for what you truly are," Grey said and took a couple swallows of the vodka. "See, bitch, I have been monitoring your calls for months now." He placed the pistol on his lap and turned the computer so she could see the screen. He showed her every phone call she made to Sunkist.

He clicked on the first recording and let it play: "I don't know where they pick the drugs up at, but I do know that Grey is pushing the work to Stanburg. Talk to you later."

She put her head down.

He went to the next recording and hit play: "I think they is on to your sister Tasha. They moved her from city to county as a transfer officer. Be careful."

"Okay, okay, I get it. So, what now, Grey? You gonna kill me and leave me behind a Dollar General too like you did Pressure?"

"No baby, not at all. Why would I do a thing like that?" He smiled and picked up his cup. "Oh, where is my manners. Would you like something to drink?"

Lopez just grilled him.

"You know what, I'm going to get you something to drink, and before you think about something stupid you should look at your phone." He got up to go get Lopez something to drink.

When he left to go to the kitchen, she got her phone out of her purse. She noticed she had one message. She quickly checked the message. What she saw broke her soul. She couldn't help but cry. The one thing she would give her life for was her daughter. Now she was being displayed on her screen. In the picture she was still asleep, but she knew somebody was in her house and her daughter was in danger. The only one that could assure her safety was Grey. She knew he was behind this shit.

She quickly took a picture of her surroundings and attached it with the picture that was sent of her daughter. She added a text: Grey's house, he got my daughter. She sent the text as Grey walked back in the living room.

"Let me see your phone," he requested. She passed him the phone with shaky hands. She just knew he was about to go through her phone. He broke the phone in half and tossed it over his shoulder. He went back in the kitchen and returned with a glass of ice.

He sat down on the couch, filled his cup back up, and filled one for Lopez. He handed her the glass. "Drink baby, tonight is about you and me. You know, on second thought I should have let you keep your phone. Who was going to call, the police?" He laughed. He leaned back on the couch. "Now, let's get this party started. Stand up for me, baby." Lopez stood up. "Now, I want to see you with your t-shirt and your panties on."

A small tear fell from the corner of her eye. She took off her shoes and slid her leggings off. Her t-shirt barely covered her ass. Grey grabbed the remote to the stereo and turned on one of his favorite slow jams, "Let's Chill" by Guy.

"You know, this song reminds me of the first time I saw you." Lopez just stood there quietly. "Dance for me, baby." Lopez moved to the center of the living room. She began to move her hips. She closed her eyes and concentrated on the music. She lifted her hands over her head. The front of her shirt slid up, revealing her panties.

Grey could feel his dick getting hard. She turned around, letting her hands down. The shirt covered her ass. "Take that shirt off." She took her shirt off, praying to God that would be all he asked of her. She let the shirt fall to the floor. Grey licked his lips. She continued to dance.

He turned up the volume. "See now, this is nice. Why does a man have to go to deep measure for motherfuckers to act right?" He took another sip of his liquor. "That's enough of that shit, take the rest of that shit off."

"Come on, Grey, don't do me like this," Lopez pleaded. The tears began to fall. Grey picked up his phone to call Stanburg. "Okay, okay, baby, whatever you want, just don't hurt my daughter." He put the phone back in his pocket.

"I will not repeat myself again tonight. Do I make myself clear?" Lopez took a deep breath and exhaled. She undid her bra and tossed it over by the rest of her clothes.

Grey watched with anticipation. Her smooth skin was like honey. She had perfect breasts, nipples the color of milk chocolate. She slid out of her panties and let them drop to the floor.

"Turn around so I can see that ass." His dick tried to jump through his pants. "Come here," he demanded. She came to him. "Get on your knees and fix it," referring to the bulge in his pants.

She undid his pants and slid his dick out of his pants. She paused to look up at him, but it only fueled his fire. He took his hand and undid her hair, letting it fall down her back. He rested his hand on the back of her head and guided her lips to the head of his dick. She took his dick in her hand and was about to go down on him. Something in her eyes must have given her away. She was going to try and bite his dick off and get his phone before he could make the call.

"Get the fuck up. You must think I'm stupid."

She got up. She wanted to run but there was nowhere to go. He was in full control. He lifted himself from the couch.

He pressed himself against her. He rubbed on her nipples while he kissed and sucked on her neck. He turned her around and bent her over the couch. She began to tremble. He ran his hand down the crease in her back. He licked his finger and massaged her asshole. He spread her legs apart. He grabbed his dick and slid the head inside her. He slowly penetrated her inch by inch until he was fully inside her.

She put her head down and gripped the back of the couch. "How do that feel, baby?" She remained quiet. "Bitch, I said how does it feel?"

"It feels good," she said in a low tone.

"That's my little bitch." He wrapped his hand in her hair and drove himself inside of her. She cried out in pain. He grabbed her by the throat with one hand and held on to her hair with the other one. Every time he penetrated her, he would choke and pull her hair back.

He finally let go of her throat and hair. He gripped her waist with both hands. He slid out of her and slapped his dick on her asshole. She jumped. "It's okay, baby, you are in good hands," he said. He picked up the Skyy vodka and poured it over her ass. The liquor ran down her back and down the crack of her ass. He sat the bottle back on the table and licked her ass while massaging her butt.

He slid his tongue down to her pussy and sucked on her clit. She was sweet. He got off his knees and positioned himself behind her. He gripped his dick and slid the head back inside her pussy. Damn, she felt so good. He slapped her across the ass, leaving his handprint on her ass.

Once his dick was fully erect, he slid off of her. He placed the head of his dick in her asshole. He stroked himself a couple of times and let the pre-nut cover her asshole. He pressed the head of his dick against her asshole.

"Please, baby, I have never done that before," she cried. Her cries fell on deaf ears.

He pressed again, spreading her cheeks apart. Damn, she was tight. He licked his finger and gently slid it inside of her. He loosened up her muscles and slid his finger out. He slid his dick between her ass cheeks a couple of times. He positioned himself behind her. He pressed the head against her asshole and the head slid in. He slid out and slid back in. This time he got about an inch.

Lopez's legs began to shake. He pressed another inch inside of her. "Oh shit…please, baby." Her cries only made him want to fuck her harder. He slapped her on the ass. He slid out of her.

"Lay on your back." She laid back on the couch. He bent down and grabbed her by the legs, pulling her to the edge of the couch. He pushed her on her back and placed her legs on his shoulders.

He slid his dick inside her and pressed her legs back to her head as he laid down on her. He reached around her legs and gripped her shoulders. He slid all the way out of her, letting his dick rest at her opening. He long-dicked her, sliding in and out of her slowly. He could feel her tightening her grip on him and knew she was about to cum. "That right, baby, cum for daddy."

He sped up the past. She turned her face. She didn't want this, but she was about to cum. She began to shake. He stroked her fast. He could feel himself about to cum. He stopped and pulled out. Her eyes popped open, wondering what happened.

"Turn around, bitch. You cum when daddy tell you to cum." She turned around.

He walked up behind her and kissed her on the back of the neck. He pulled her hair, causing her to put an arch in her back. It also caused her to tilt her ass up, giving Grey what he was looking for. With his free hand he gripped his dick and slid inside her from the back as they both stood. He began to penetrate her as he talked to her.

"I have waited my whole life to enjoy myself inside of you. Now, tell me you love this dick"

"I love this dick," she cried.

"I can't hear you."

"I love this dick," she shouted.

He fucked her harder. "I'm not going to lie," he whispered in her ear, "you got the best pussy I ever had." He fucked her harder. They made their way from the couch to the living room wall. She placed both hands on the wall as Grey drove inside her.

Her legs began to shake, but she remained quiet. He grabbed her hair with one hand and placed the other on her stomach. Her body began to tremble. Grey could feel the sensation traveling down his spine into the shaft of his dick. She bit down on her lip, trying to hold back her orgasm. "Now, cum for me, bitch." And with those words she erupted. Grey gripped her body with both hands as he came inside her.

"Oh shit…ummm…shit…awww." She looked up to the heavens and asked God why this had to happen to her.

Grey slid out of her and whispered in her ear, "The sex was great." He reached around her head and broke her neck. "Bitch, if I can't have you, no one will." He retrieved his phone and called Stanburg. He immediately picked up.

"Yes, boss?"

"Send a cleanup over and kill the kid in her sleep. We will make it look like they went on vacation."

"Will do, sir. Talk to you later," Stanburg said.

Grey ended the call.

CHAPTER 37

It was 12:30 p.m. Sunday afternoon. The sun was high in the sky. The weather was nice.

Killa pulled into the McDonald's drive-through. He hadn't eaten breakfast and his stomach was touching his back. He pulled in line behind a Chevrolet Trailblazer. As he waited to order his food he listened to the radio. He switched cars every day, but the 2021 Dodge Durango SRT Hellcat he rented for today had him thinking about buying it. His stomach started to growl. Damn, this line slow as hell. He was about to back up and go somewhere else until a GMC Yukon pulled in behind him. Man, this shit is crazy, he thought.

He slid down in his seat. He turned the radio off 'cause they were playing a bullshit mix. Damn, 'bout time. He pulled up to order his food. "Welcome to McDonald's, how may I help you?"

"Let me get a number one with extra cheese and onions."

"What would you like to drink, sir."

"Let me get a sweet tea and a apple pie."

"Will that be all?"

"Yeah, that'll be it."

"Your total is $7.21. Pull up to the first window."

His phone rang. He answered it without checking the number. "Yo, hold on for a sec," he told the caller while he pulled up to the first window.

He smiled when he saw Meeka. "Hey, Killa, how you been, boo?"

"Shit, just trying to make a dollar out of 15 cent," Killa said.

"That's good, and your total is $7.21." He paid for his food and pulled to the second window.

"Yo, sorry about that. Who dis?"

"So, do all your little groupies be calling you that or are you just a dog?" Candy asked.

"I can't help how people feel about me, but it takes a dog to know one."

"I don't know, I don't fuck with dogs. I can't get accustomed to fleas. Let talk about what's relevant, like you buying my dress."

"Straightforward, I like that. Do you want me to pick you up or do you want to meet me?"

"I will meet you, of course. Where at?"

"Kickback Jack's in an hour, and make sure you brush your teeth."

"Tell your mama."

"See you there." Killa ended the call. He got his food and placed it in the passenger seat.

He had a couple of rounds to make before he met up with Candy. His first stop would be in the Heights. He had to pick up 10 brandz from Boogotti and drop off four birdz to his brother Long Head. Then he had to pull up on Progress Street to holla at lil Buck. He just came home and was looking to get on.

He looked at the clock on the dash. It read 1 p.m. He had to pull everything together by 2:00. He couldn't wait to see Candy again.

CHAPTER 38

The private plane touched down at her new residence. "Oh my God, this is beautiful, Zi." Fire had her face pressed against the window trying to see the rest of the estate.

Zionna was happy she liked it. "Girl, wait until you see the inside," Zionna said, joining her by the window.

Fire gave her sister a hug. "Thank you so much, sis."

The plane landed and Fire was the first one off. The mansion sat in the middle of the woods and isolated from any road for two miles. The lawn was manicured with a wraparound driveway. The mansion was built with black and grey keystone. The driveway was an off-grey that accommodated the mansion.

There was a lake and a boating dock. There was a large pool and basketball court. Fire was in heaven and started to cry. She quickly wiped her tears away.

"Let's go inside," Zionna said, passing Fire the key to the house.

They made their way to the front door. Fire unlocked the door and they went in. Zionna closed the door behind them. The mansion was exquisite, completely indelible. Fire stood in the middle of the floor and relished the beauty of the mansion. High ceilings, two stairways to the upper level. Wash-grey colored walls. Black and grey checker flooring.

She ran upstairs to check out the rest of the house. There was a master bedroom to her left and two other rooms to her right.

"Let me show you something," Zionna said as she reached the top of the stairs. Fire followed her sister as she opened one of the doors to her right. They stepped in the room and Zi turned on the light.

"The room was built and specialized for a baby boy. The room beside this one is for a girl, so no matter what you have their room is already ready whenever or if you choose to have kids."

Fire ran her hand over the small blanket that laid in the crib. This was a dream come true and she couldn't wait to start a life with her one and only love.

"How can I ever repay, sis?" Fire held back the tears.

"You can repay me by living the life I took from you."

They embraced each other and finally Fire broke down and cathartically she released all of her pent-up emotions. Zionna held her as she cried in her arms.

She needed the support of her sister and Zionna wouldn't fail her twice. They looked identical but were as different as water and oil. Zionna finally saw her sister for who she really was. She was a delicate flower that just wanted her sister's approval that she wasn't a failure.

Fire's phone rang. She pulled herself together so she could take the call. She pulled the phone out of her pocket and checked the number. Her world lit up once she saw it was Sunkist. "Hey, baby!"

"What's good, love? How you been holding up?"

"I'm good now that I have heard from you. You had me a little worried, but I know you needed time to get yourself together mentally, physically, and emotionally."

"That is exactly what I did. I came out here to the Philippines to holla at the plug and clear my mind. Baby, I wish I could be there with you, but due to the circumstances I can't."

"Baby, I'm coming to get you. I would have you come to me but where I'm located there is no address. This place doesn't exist."

"Baby, you got me confuse, but I trust you, and why do I feel like Zionna got something to do with this?"

"Well, look at the time. Text me your location and we will be there."

"We! I knew it, but I'm sending you the address now. But you stay put and let Zionna come to get me, plus there is something we need to talk about."

"Okay, cool. Hope to see you soon. I love you."

"I love you too," Sunkist said. Fire ended the call.

CHAPTER 39

Killa pulled up to his crib in Aaron Lakes. He had to drop off the money he had collected. He parked his car and hopped out, leaving the car running. He looked at his watch: 1:50 p.m. He had only 10 minutes to spare before he had to go meet up with Candy. He ran in the crib to make sure nothing was out of place. He ran over to the kitchen and opened the cabinet. He snatched out a box of Frosted Flakes, opened the box, and dumped out the money.

He counted out five grand and put the rest back. He put the money in his pocket and put the box of cereal back in the cabinet. He locked up behind him and ran back to his car, jumped in, and pulled off.

He was just passing Cross Creek Mall when his phone rang. He looked at the caller ID and saw it was Candy. He answered the call. "I'm about to pull in now. What kind of car you in?"

"I'm in a Cadillac Escalade ESV."

"Okay, I see you." Killa ended the call. He pulled up beside her and parked. He got out and waited for Candy to join him.

Candy stepped out of the Cadillac Escalade in full fashion. She sported a Dolce & Gabbana miniskirt designed with black and white squares with a matching shirt and black and white retro Jordans. Her black hair was done in an up-do with white highlights. She was naturally beautiful with no makeup.

"So, are we going in or are you going to keep staring at me?"

Killa had gotten lost in her beauty. She was not your ordinary young girl. To be pushing a whip like that her people had to be paid and judging by her dress code she had swag. "Baby, the only thing I stare at is dollar sign. Ladies first."

Candy led the way inside Kickback Jack's. The atmosphere was nice and at this time of the day it wasn't too crowded. Killa got a table for two and they made their way to their seats. Candy put her phone on the table and got herself comfortable. Killa sat down and grabbed the menu. He had just eaten so he was just grabbing some cheese fries.

Candy had been here a couple of times and already knew what she wanted.

"I'm gonna get some cheese fries. What do you want?"

"I'm gonna get the Philly cheesesteak," she said, then licked her lips.

"Hi, my name is Kelly and I will be your waiter this afternoon. Are y'all ready to order?"

"Yes, we are. I will like a single order of cheese fries and my lady will have a Philly cheesesteak."

"Would y'all like anything to drink?"

"I'll take a fruit punch," Killa said.

"I will have a glass of water," Candy announced.

"Be back shortly." The waiter left.

Killa chose to initiate the conversation. "So, Miss Candy, where are you from?"

"I'm from here, born and raised."

"Word! What school did you go to?"

"I went to Southview," Candy said. "What school did you go to?"

"I went to E.E. Smith. I grow up on the Murk, so you already know how that goes," Killa said.

"Trust and believe I do," Candy said. She hated the Murk. It was a shithole and nothing good came out of it. The neighborhoods were drug infested, people sucking and fucking for a damn rock. Shit was crazy. She didn't judge those that hustle because if she did hustle, she damn sure would be the hustler and not the customer.

"So, Mr. Killa, what do you do for a living?" she asked with a smirk on her face waiting for him to lie.

"I'm a product of my environment, so I sell product to the environment."

She was at a loss for words. He was completely honest. For the first time she really looked at him. He was well-dressed, his hair was cut neatly, and his cold, black skin was smooth. He had white teeth and clean fingernails. Most of all, he wasn't a liar. Killa had her respect.

"Thank you for being open and honest. To be real, I thought you was gonna sit up here and lie directly to my face, and when you did, you would have never saw me again."

The waiter brought them their drinks to the table.

"Thank you," Candy said as she took her glass of water. Killa sat his drink on the table.

"So, what do you do, Ms. Candy?"

"I am an exotic dancer."

Killa's eyes popped open and Candy almost fell out of her seat from laughing so hard. She was in tears. "Boy! If you could have seen the look on your face. Ha-ha!"

"Hell, that shit ain't funny." Killa didn't find that shit funny at all.

"Aww, I'm sorry if I made you feel some type of way." She rubbed the side of his face. He couldn't help but smile.

The waiter brought their food. They ate in silence. Candy kept catching Killa staring at her. "Something on you mind?" she finally broke the silence.

"I just want to tell you that I think you are gorgeous."

She blushed. "Thank you."

They finished their meal and Killa paid the bill, leaving a $20 tip. "Since the mall is across the street, do you want to hit the mall to see if there is anything you like?" Killa asked.

"Killa! That dress cost me four grand. What can Cross Creek Mall do for me?" She smiled.

Killa reached in his pocket and pulled out the five grand. "It's not what the mall can do, it's what I can do for you." He tossed her the roll of money. She took the money and put it in her purse.

"I see you are a man of your word. Hit me up tonight around 9 if you not busy." She gave him a hug.

Killa couldn't help but to palm her ass. "See, I give you a inch and you take a mile," she said. She got in her SUV and pulled off.

CHAPTER 40

John Charles and Sunkist waited for Zionna to arrive. They sat in a black BMW M440i xDrive about 20 yards away from his landing strip.

As they waited, they talked business. John Charles had been his plug for many years, but their relationship was far past money. John Charles became his mentor and his friend. "Sunkist, I want you to think about leaving the game. You are your own man, and you make your own decisions. By all means, I am with you no matter what your choices are. Remember, there is no longevity in the dope game. I would love for this to be the last time we see each other on terms of business. If you ever need me, I am a phone call away."

"I appreciate that, old man." Both men smiled, enjoying each other's company.

A small jet was coming into view. Sunkist shook Charles' hand. "Thank you for everything." Sunkist opened the car door and got out. The heat from the sun hit him directly in the face. He shut the car door behind him.

Zionna's private jet landed. After a minute or so the door to the jet opened and Zi peeked her head out from the doorway. She motioned him to come on. He boarded the jet, and they took off.

Sunkist looked around the jet making sure Fire wasn't on the jet. Zionna knew him well. "You don't have to worry, she stayed in the states so you can relax."

He exhaled. "Thanks for coming to get me."

"No problem," she replied.

"This is the shit I want to holla at you about." Sunkist pulled out his phone. He went into his messages and pulled up the last message that Lopez sent him. He showed the pictures to Zionna.

She took the phone and viewed the contents. The first picture was of someone's living room. She looked closely at the picture and there was a picture of police chief Grey in uniform hanging on the wall. This has to be Grey's crib, she thought. She looked at the second picture. This picture was of a child about 12 or 13 years of age. The child looked to be asleep. "Who is the little girl?" Zionna asked.

"That is Lopez's youngest daughter Mylasha."

Zionna read the text message that was attached. "Look like to me either Grey is blackmailing her, or he is going to use her to get to one of us."

"Something ain't right 'cause Grey never gives his home address to anyone outside of the black ops officials under his control. The only one that has his home address is the mother of his kids and she won't break, not even for her sister. See, Koontz's loyalty is to him but I was fucking with her on some other shit. I use to pay her for information and to get my homies off when she was assistant D.A., but once she met Grey her loyalty became unbalanced and her view changed of us. I had ties to Lopez and Koontz still did business with me on the strength of her sister."

"I see now, but what do you think Grey is up to?" Zionna asked.

"Shit, I don't know, but it ain't good. See, for Lopez to send them pictures like she did she was scared and wanted her whereabouts to be known."

"So, how do you want to play this? This nigga Grey is coming for all of us and even I lay in the balance," Zionna said.

"You are right. There is no telling the intel he has on us and who we are associated with, especially now that he has Lopez. She is strong but will break under the threat of her children safety," Sunkist said. "I never put all my eggs in one basket, though. I got Trearina on Sgt. Toney Jones as we speak. See, as long as Grey and Stanburg feel we have left Fayetteville and went into hiding they will let their guard down, and when they do, I will be there." Sunkist laid his head back and closed his eyes.

CHAPTER 41

She sat in the driveway across from officer Sgt. Toney James' house. Trearina had been following him for the last week. She knew what time his wife came home, what time she left to pick up their baby from her sister's house, what time she got back from fucking her ex. Most of all she knew that she left to take her son to see his father on Tuesday and Thursday nights around 9 p.m.

She had strict orders from Sunkist to call Lil Don when the time was right. She looked at her watch, it was 7:45 p.m. She pulled out her phone to call Lil Don. He picked up on the first ring.

"What's good, Tee?"

"It's time. I'm going to text you the address to the spot. I'm going to go ahead and go in the crib and wait until he come home. Once wifey and the kid come in, I will open the back door for you to come in."

"Say no more."

Trearina ended the call. She slid down in her seat and waited.

CHAPTER 42

Nine o'clock came quickly. Killa was playing Fortnite on the PlayStation 4. He looked at his watch. Oh shit! He put the game on pause. He pulled his phone out to call Candy. She picked up on the second ring.

"Hello!"

"What's good? You busy?"

"Nah, I'm just doing my toes right now."

"Can I pull up or you want to wait until another time 'cause I know how much time you gonna have to put in on them monsters."

"Boy, shut up, I ain't got no ugly feet and if I did you would still suck on them."

"Alright then, I'm on my way. Just send me your location. Do you want me to pick up anything along the way?"

"Pick up some condoms."

There was a pause before Killa responded.

"A'ight, cool."

"Let me stop playing with you. I forgot you are the serious type, but you can pick up some blunts."

"Fo show, be there in a minute."

Candy ended the call and sent a text with the address to one of her friends at work. Little did Killa know he would never have her address. After she sent Killa the address she sent out another text and tossed the phone on the couch. She went into the bathroom to check herself in the mirror.

She had on a dark red Ramy Brook Julianne midi-dress. She let her hair down. She licked her lips with self-approval. It's a damn shame to look this good, she thought as she left the bathroom.

She went into the kitchen to see what type of liquor her friend had to drink. She opened the champagne cabinet. A full bottle of Maestro Dobel tequila caught her attention. She took the bottle out. She went to the kitchen cabinet and pulled out some shot glasses for her and Killa. She went to her purse and got the ounce of Girl Scout weed. She brought everything into the living room. She sat on the couch and waited for Killa to arrive.

Killa pulled up in Tiffany Pines around 9:30 p.m. He followed his GPS until it announced, "You have arrived at your destination." He parked the Dodge Durango, grabbed the blunts, and got out. He hit the alarm and adjusted his pistol in his waist. He walked up and rang the doorbell.

"Who is it?" Candy asked.

"Your daddy. Now, come open the door."

Candy opened the door. "First of all, I never knew my daddy. I only know my mother, so don't speak of him in that way ever again. Do we have an understanding?" Candy said seriously. She was blocking the doorway waiting for Killa to say he understood.

"Yeah ma, I got you, shit. I know how you feel, I never knew mine either."

She let down her guard and let him in. She closed the door. "Did you get the blunts, Killa?" she said as she went into the kitchen to get some ice for their drinks.

"Yeah, I got them." Killa picked up the bag of weed. "Damn, this shit loud. What kind of loud is this?" Killa asked.

"That is Girl Scout but I mixed it with Daydream." Candy came back into the living room. She sat on the couch and poured their drinks while Killa rolled up.

Once the blunt was rolled, Killa lit it and took a couple of pulls. He inhaled the last pull and held the weed smoke in his lungs for a moment before exhaling. "Yo, this shit is good," Killa said while passing the blunt.

Candy passed him his shot of liquor. She took the blunt and hit it a few times and passed it back. She threw back her first shot and refilled her glass.

Killa hit the blunt and passed it back. He took his shot. "So, how was your day, baby girl?" Killa asked.

"My day was actually great. I had a good time with a so-far nice guy. What more can a girl ask for?" Candy said with a bright smile on her face.

"Well, I'm glad you enjoyed yourself and hopefully you will allow me to be a part of your life."

"We will see how things go," Candy said.

Killa got up and came to sit beside her. He picked up the bottle of liquor and poured her another shot and handed it to her.

She smiled at him, knowing what he was trying to do. She took the shot glass and sat it down on the table. "Your ass ain't smooth. You think you going to get me drunk and then get some pussy, huh?"

Killa knew he was busted. "Baby, believe me…." He stopped before he finished his sentence. He knew she was hip to his game, so he decided to just tell her how he really felt. He got closer to her. His closeness made her nervous but at the same time she wanted his touch.

Killa put his hand on her thigh. She didn't resist his touch. Killa leaned in to whisper in her ear. "To be honest, you are irresistible to me. The pure essence of your beauty is intoxicating. Your eyes, your smell, the softness of your skin." Killa moved his hand up a little, raising up her midi-dress. He continued to whisper in her ear, letting himself capture her mind. "I want to enter your world. I want to be become a part of your thought process. Let me be there for you."

Her mind was racing and her heart was running laps. She had to stop him before she gave in, but she was getting weaker by the second.

Killa kissed her on the neck and slid his hand up her midi-dress. She wasn't wearing any panties. Killa continued to kiss her on the neck as he ran his fingers between her pussy lips.

A fire of desire shot through her entire body. She bit down on her lip, enjoying the connection.

Killa found her clit and began to massage it. She opened her legs to give him access. She moaned, "It feels so good, Killa."

He dropped to his knees and grabbed her by her legs and pulled her to the edge of the couch. She laid back and placed one leg up on the table so Killa could eat her pussy.

Killa pulled his gun from his waist and slit it under the couch. She placed a hand on the top of Killa's head and guided him to her pussy.

Her pussy was pretty. Killa began to lick and suck on her clit. She closed her eyes. "Umm, baby…ummm…stay right there."

Killa took two fingers and slid them inside her as he ate her pussy. He found her G-spot and began to stroke her. She arched her back. "Oh God, yes, baby…yes." She began to ride his face. He licked his pointer finger and massaged the rim of her asshole. He sucked on her clit and she wrapped her legs around his head. He slid his finger in her asshole while eating her pussy and stroking her G-spot.

Oh shit…what…the fuck is…he…doing to me? "Oh God! Please don't stop." She grabbed one of the couch cushions and placed it over her mouth. "Baby, I'm about to cum." With all of her strength she had in her body she latched down on Killa's face and exploded. She rocked him for a moment, grinding her pussy in his face. After she exhaled, she collapsed.

Killa smiled, knowing she was satisfied. Killa began to undress. She put one foot up on the couch and played with her pussy while watching Killa undress.

Killa laid down on top of her and kissed her lips. She slid her tongue in his mouth while he played with her nipples. Killa couldn't take no more, he had to be inside her. He reached between his legs and grabbed his dick. He tried to slide inside her and she stopped him.

"Do you have protection?" Candy asked.

"Nah, but we good, baby." Killa tried to slide inside of her again.

"Nigga, what don't you understand about me saying 'protection'?" She was starting to get upset.

"Damn, baby, I don't have any condoms."

"Look, I got some in the bedroom, just go get them. First bedroom on the left."

Killa hopped up to go get the condom. Once Killa was out of sight she quickly got dressed. "Baby, where they at?" Killa yelled from the bedroom.

"In the top drawer." She grabbed her purse and phone and opened the door for Stanburg. Stanburg stepped in and closed the door.

"Where is he?" She pointed down the hall towards the bedroom. Stanburg slid up against the living room wall and waited for Killa to appear.

Killa couldn't find the condoms, so he decided he would have to make a trip to the store to grab a box. He left the bedroom and walked into the living room, walking past Stanburg. He noticed Candy was fully dressed and was standing by the front door, like she was ready to leave.

"What's good, Candy, you…." Click!

"Don't move, motherfucker."

Killa couldn't comprehend what was going on. "Get on your knees," Stanburg screamed.

"Fuck you! I don't get on my knees for no one," Killa spat.

Stanburg laughed at his statement. "That's funny, you got on your knees for that one," pointing the gun in officer Martinez's direction.

That shit killed him inside. She had played him.

Stanburg hit Killa in the back of the head with the 357 revolver, dropping him to his knees. "You are free to go, officer Martinez. I got it from here."

Martinez's heart went out to Killa. She took one last look at Killa, opened the door, and left.

"I'm going to give you one more chance to come clean and I promise you on my kid's life, you will be a free man. I will give you a million in cash and that woman that just walked out of here will be yours. All you have to do is give us Sunkist."

"Seven the hard way, motherfucker. Suck my dick."

"Wrong choice, boy." Boom! Killa's body fell to the floor. Blood spattered all over the living room. Stanburg wiped his face, removing parts of brain fragments. He cleaned his pistol with his shirt and placed it back on his hip.

He reached down and searched Killa. He found Killa's phone. He hit the power button and the screen lit up. "Stupid motherfucker," Stanburg said once he saw the phone was unlocked. He went to the contacts and saw the contact for Sunkist. Bingo! He put the phone in his pocket.

He had a plan. He would meet with Peterson and work a deal with him so he would eliminate Grey and appoint him as the H.N.I.C. of Cumberland County. He was tired of doing all the work while Grey reaped all the benefits. Now that he could eliminate Sunkist the game was his and his alone.

He pulled out his phone to call the cleanup crew. He walked over to the table, picked up the bottle of liquor, and poured himself a few shots. Cheers to a better life.

CHAPTER 43

Trearina had almost fallen asleep when Meagan pulled out the driveway. She waited a couple of seconds to make sure Meaghan was gone. She looked at her watch and saw it was 8:05 p.m. She had time to execute her plan.

She put her gloves on and grabbed a crowbar out of her trunk. She shut her trunk, looked around to make sure no one was outside. Cliffdale Forest was a quiet neighborhood with not a lot of traffic along the back side of the neighborhood. She crossed the street and jumped the gate that surrounded the backyard. She scanned the backyard for a dog before she moved.

She moved to the back door. She tried the door, but it was locked. She looked under the doormat for a spare key. No luck. She ran her hand along the top ledge of the door frame. Bingo! She took the key and unlocked the door.

She quickly scanned the house. It was empty. There was a door beside the back door. She opened it to see what was inside. It was a food pantry. She began to rearrange the pantry so she could fit inside it. Once the space was clear she texted Lil Don and told him she was in. She slid the phone back in her pocket.

She went to the living room and sat on a couch. She would wait for them to arrive. As the time passed, she played with the baby 380. So pretty, yet so deadly. She popped the clip out and checked the clip. After examination, she popped it back in and cocked it back. She laid the gun on the couch and got up.

She walked over to a shelf that displayed a few pictures. Sgt. Toney Jones was in one picture in full uniform. In another picture of him and Meagan were all hugged up. Trearina put that picture face down. There were a couple more pictures of family and friends.

There was a car pulling in the driveway. She ran to the window to look out. Meagan was carrying the baby, but Jones was nowhere in sight. Fuck! She ran and snatched the gun off the couch and made it to the pantry just in time. Trearina had the pantry door cracked so she could see out the door.

Meagan came in the house talking on the phone and carrying her baby. She closed the door behind her. She laid the baby on the couch and came into the kitchen. "I'm about to get dinner started and will see you in a few." Meagan ended the call and put her phone on the kitchen counter.

Meagan went back in the living room. She picked up her son and went upstairs. Trearina slid out the pantry and ran over and got Meagan's phone. She checked to see if it had a lock on it. The phone was unlocked. Trearina checked the last person she called, and it was Jones. She put the phone down and slid back into the pantry. She cracked the door as Meagan came back in the kitchen.

Meagan pulled out two pots and a pan from the cabinet under the sink. She went to the fridge and got two steaks and put them in the sink. She cut the water on in the sink so the water could run over the frozen steaks. She was coming towards the pantry.

Trearina's heart began to pump. She gripped the pistol out of fear. Meagan placed her hand on the doorknob to the pantry. Trearina lifted the gun. Meagan's phone rang. Meagan went to answer her phone. "Hello?"

"I'm about to come by to see my son. Are you home?"

"Yes, I am home."

"Okay, I will see you in a few."

Meagan ended the call. She dialed another number and waited for them to answer. Trearina heard her say that Jones was coming over so after he left they would just go out to eat. Meagan ended the call. She turned off the water and threw the steaks in the trash. She was pissed.

Her baby's father was becoming a thorn in her side. It was like he knew every time she was about to meet her ex. She couldn't take this shit no more. She was going to tell Jones that their relationship is over, that she's not in love with him anymore. Sure, she still cared about him, but the sex was getting just plain whack plus he'd been cheating on her for the last year with that little bitch Kimberly that works down at the post office. He had played her for a fool, but she would have the last laugh.

She went to check on her son. Trearina's phone vibrated. She pulled her phone from out of her pocket. She had a message from Lil Don. She checked the message: We are here, parked across the street. She quickly texted back: Come to the back door now, his girl is upstairs with the baby.

Trearina slid out of the pantry and stopped to listen to see if she could hear any movement coming from upstairs. Once the coast was clear, she opened the back door. Lil Don was the first one through the door followed by Sumo, Lil Weezy, Tiny Harlem, BK Red, Smooth, Father, and Sandman. They were masked up and had their guns drawn.

"Look, she is upstairs, and Sgt. Jones is on his way over here now," Trearina informed them.

"A'ight, we got it from here," Lil Don said.

Trearina shot out the back door, glad to get the hell out of there. She ran all the way back to her car, hopped in, and sped off.

Lil Don locked the back door. "Yo Tiny Harlem, make sure the front door is locked." Lil Don picked up Meagan's phone off the counter and put it in his pocket. Lil Don slid out a chair from the kitchen table. "Smooth, Lil Weezy, and BK Red, bring that bitch to me," Lil Don ordered.

They made their way upstairs. Meagan was in her bedroom changing her clothes when they entered her bedroom.

"Oh my God, please don't hurt me," she said while trying to cover herself.

"Get dressed and do what we say and you are good. No harm will come to you or your baby," Lil Weezy said. "Now, if you choose the alternative route, that pretty white skin of yours is gonna be an ashy grey. You feel me?"

Lil Weezy picked up the baby to make sure he had her full cooperation. "I will do whatever y'all want," she said, her eyes bouncing from one to the other, "but please don't rape me."

"Man, shut the fuck up, plus you ain't even like that. Now, get your silly ass downstairs," Father barked, feeling disrespected by Meagan's words. What the fuck is wrong with these white girls out here? First thing that comes to mind is please don't rape me. Bitches done bumped their heads, but shit. If you was in my house and I was a woman with eight other people with guns out I wouldn't know what to expect either. I can see her point of view, Father thought.

They made their way downstairs to join Lil Don and Sandman. "Have a seat Ms. Meagan." Lil Don stood, allowing Meagan to sit down. "I know you are confused and don't know what is going on right now, so let me explain," Lil Don said while pulling out another chair from the kitchen table. He placed the chair directly in front of her and sat down.

"Your man and the father of your child is a corrupt cop and is conspiring with other corrupted officials to kill and eliminate us for their beneficial gain. Now, you know this is a eat or get ate world that we live in. Either you are the predator or the prey, and in this situation, I don't want you to be leftovers."

Meagan's phone rang. Lil Don took the phone out of his pocket. He held it up so Meagan could see the number. "Do you recognize this number?" Lil Don said.

"That's him calling me now," she said.

"Okay, I want you to answer the phone and play cool. Get him over here if he is not already on his way." Lil Don passed her the phone.

She answered. "Hello."

"I'm pulling up now," Jones said.

"I'm in the kitchen cooking, you can let yourself in."

"Okay."

"Okay, bye." Meagan ended the call. "He is about to pull up now," she said.

"A'ight, look, Sumo and BK Red post up on the stairs. Tiny Harlem, you and Sandman post up behind the couch. Father, post up in the hall closet. I'm gonna post up here in the pantry," Lil Don said. "Meagan, you act like you are about to cook." Lil Don got the baby from Lil Weezy and everybody took their posts.

Meagan got up, wiping the tears from her eyes. She didn't know what was about to happen, but she had to think about the safety of her son, and if that meant doing what they said, so be it. She went to the sink to wash her hands. She could hear the front door being unlocked and she knew it was Jones. Her heart began to race. The door opened.

"Meagan, where you at?"

"I'm in the kitchen, I told you I was cooking."

Jones shut the door and immediately felt something wasn't right. It was too late. Everyone stepped out with their guns drawn. Sumo slid to the front door and locked it. Lil Don stepped out of the pantry holding Jones' son in his arms.

"Mr. Jones, come on in and join us," Lil Don said. Jones walked slowly to the kitchen.

"What is this all about?" Jones said, acting dumb to the facts.

"We will get to all that, Mr. Jones, but first have a seat," Lil Don said pointing to the chair he had placed in front of Meagan only moments ago. Jones took the chair and turned it around so he could face Lil Don. He sat down.

"Get something to tie him up." Father had seen a couple of electric cords when he was in the closet. Father ran to the closet and got the cords. He tied Jones' hands and feet together.

"Meagan, come and have a seat by your man." She rolled her eyes at Jones. She sat down in the chair and Father tied her up as well.

Lil Don handed Lil Weezy the baby. "Mr. Jones, you act surprised to see us. Oh, that's right, you don't know us 'cause your daddies Grey and Stanburg don't know us. So, let me introduce myself. My name is Sunkist, my name is Fire, Pressure, Killa…we are one. So, now that we have been introduced, we can be gangstas about this or it can get real bloody in this bitch, your choice. I'm going to ask you a few questions and you will answer my questions. If you lie, you will not have a chance to tell the truth, Mr. Jones, without sacrificing something. Now, my first question is simple. Where is the money and the drugs at?" Lil Don said, rubbing his hands together.

"I don't have no…." Before he could finish his sentence Lil Don pulled his strap. "I don't have money here, but I have $600,000 in a safe at my house and 70 bricks in the attic. If I give you that, will you let me and my family go?"

"You say $600,000 and 70 bricks? We may just be able to arrange something. Hold on for a second." Lil Don pulled out his cell and called Sunkist. He picked up immediately.

"Hz, homie."

"Yo, I got this nigga Jones tied up, him and his wife. I got their baby too but check this. I was just gonna kill the nigga after we got the info but he offering 600,000 and 70 bricks for him and his family freedom."

"That is a lot of money, my G. A'ight, look, put the baby in the oven and cut it on. Tell him you want Stanburg's address to his home. If he truly love his family he will come off the address. Once we have the address, we will work the deal with him for the 600,000 and 70 bricks if he helps us grab Stanburg. We will hold Meagan and the kid until everything is finished."

"Fo show, say no more." Lil Don ended the call.

"Today is your lucky day, Mr. Jones. We got a deal for the 600,000 and 70 bricks for you and your family freedom but as we do you this favor, we ask for one in return."

"And what that might be?" Jones asked.

"You will give us your superior Captain Stanburg's address."

"I don't have it. The only one that has it is Grey," Jones said.

Lil Don walked over to Lil Weezy and got the baby from him. He then walked over to the oven, opened the door, and placed the baby inside. Lil Don shut the door and cut the oven on.

"Oh my God, my baby!" Meagan screamed.

"Okay, okay, I will give you the address, just take my son out of there."

Lil Don cut the oven off and took the baby out. "You play a dangerous game, Mr. Jones," Lil Don said. "Now, you will help us grab Stanburg. Once we have him, we will let your girl and baby go, but we will hold them now for insurance. Sumo and BK Red, take Mr. Jones to pick up the money and the work. I will get your number from Meagan. We will be in touch, Mr. Jones."

CHAPTER 44

Fire was standing on the manicured grass watching the jet come into view. She couldn't wait to wrap her arms around Sunkist. God, she missed him. Lately it felt like her soul was mingling, trying to reattach itself. Sunkist was her soulmate and without him she was incomplete. It took everything in her not to follow him but with the simple momentary thought that she would follow him to the grave.

The private jet landed. The weather was nice. The heat index was low, and the wind was cool. As the jet door opened, Fire stood excited, eager to embrace her love.

Sunkist appeared and she ran to him with open arms. Once Sunkist reached the bottom step Fire jumped in his arms. She needed him more than he could ever comprehend. She buried her face into his shoulder blades and her body began to trembly with emotions.

Sunkist was silent and just held her. He had never seen this side of her. He was familiar with the complete opposite. Her being fearless, strong, and sustainable against the worst. He could feel the dampness of her tears on his neck and knew she was just a woman that needed to be loved. He felt he had to be accountable for half of her pain and it killed him inside. She held him in high regard and honored the ground he walked on. It was time to show his appreciation for the love and support she gave him.

"Baby, I have decided to leave the streets once the opposition has met his demise." Fire immediately stopped crying and stepped back from him. She searched his face for any signs of deception. A smile illuminated her face.

"You are serious," she said.

"On my trip to the Philippines I had the chance to put some things into a better perspective and now that I have my priorities right, I know what I have to do." He got down on one knee and took Fire's hand in his. "Ms. Unique Nicole Spellmen, will you make me the happiest man in the world? Will you marry me?"

"Yes, baby, yes, I will marry you." She looked over at her sister. "Zionna, I'm getting married."

Zionna struggled to keep her tears back. She was extremely happy for them and knew she did the right thing by giving them her estate. Zionna kissed her sister and gave Sunkist a warm hug. She said her goodbyes and boarded the jet to return to New York.

"Come on, baby, let me show you our new home." Fire took Sunkist by the hand, and they made their way around the mansion. Sunkist was at a loss for words. The place was absolutely beautiful. The scent of pine trees lingered in the air, giving the smell of the countryside. The air was clean and the environment was calm and peaceful. He could definitely get used to this. The place was breathtaking, especially the water on the lake. He could picture himself fishing and taking late night boat rides on the river. Him making love to Unique under the moonlight.

Fire politely tapped his shoulder, bringing him back to reality, relieving him of his fantasy. He briefly stared at her curiously.

"Come on, baby, let's go inside," she shouted. She was halfway across the yard by the time his recollection came back. By the time he made it to the front door Fire was dancing and singing in the middle of the floor. This was a sight to see. "Come on, baby, dance with me."

He walked over casually and took her hand in his. They began to dance together. Fire led and he followed. They danced to the rhythm of their heartbeats. He stared into her dazzling eyes and saw the inevitable—he was lost without her. The flawlessness of her beauty hypnotized him, leaving him under her spell. He held on to her as if he let go she would vanish.

She rubbed the side of his face and broke their embrace. "Come on, I got to show you the rest of the house," she snickered. She ran up the steps to the upper level. Sunkist followed her. Once they were upstairs Fire showed him the two baby rooms and led him to the master bedroom. She opened the bedroom door. "Look at the size of it, baby. We got a balcony with a view of the lake. We got a walk-in bath surrounded by glass and look at the size of this bed."

She ran and jumped on the bed. She turned onto her stomach and rested her head on her hands. "So, what do you think, baby?" Fire said, letting her dreads fall in her face.

"To be honest, I love it." Sunkist kicked off his shoes and laid down on the bed beside her. He took his hand and slid her dreads behind her ear. "You are so beautiful." She smiled flirtatiously. He admired her beauty, concealing his true intentions. His expression emphasized lust while consistently holding his emotions in check. There was something in her eyes that abandoned any restraints. She wanted to be captured.

He leaned in to kiss her and she accepted him willingly. The passion between them was radiating through their connection. He slid his tongue in her mouth and they began to French kiss. His hands escaped to roam her body. He sucked on her neck and caressed her breasts. She squirmed under his embrace. He was eager to get inside her, but he took his time, pleasantly feeling the softness of her skin. The touch of her alone was electric.

He began to pull at her shirt. She quickly removed it and tossed it to the floor. He undid her bra and let it fall to the bed. She had the most perfect breasts. He caressed and massaged both nipples until they were fully erect. He began to suck on her nipple. He began to undress as she laid on her back. He tossed his shirt on the floor and quickly removed his pants, tossing them off the bed.

He laid on top of her. They continued to engage in foreplay. He ran his hands through her locks. She slid down his boxer shorts. He completed the task, letting them drop at the end of the bed. She slid out of her shirt and tossed it to the floor. Her panties were soaked. He relieved her of them and threw them over his shoulder. He was honored to share this experience.

She laid back on the bed. He ran his hand down her stomach, feeling the tightness of her body. He felt her legs and thighs. The softness had him fully erect. He slid down between her legs so he could please her.

She stopped him. She pulled him up. "I want you inside of me," she whispered.

He straddled her. His dick invaded her private area. She spread her legs, giving him her approval. She became submissive and let go. He guided his shaft to her opening and penetrated her. She wrapped her legs around him as he slid inside her. "Ummm…," she exhaled.

She stared into his eyes, and they became one. She became fragile under his control. He proceeded with caution. Her pussy was tight, like fucking a virgin for the first time, but the more he gave her, the more she loosened up. He was almost fully inside her, and with one long, deep stroke he completed his mission.

She cried out his name and dug her nails deep into his back. Her femininity consumed him, and he lost control. He slid back in her more forcefully. "Oh, baby," she cried out. She began to push away. He laid his weight down on her, pinning her to the mattress. He lifted her leg and drove deep inside her.

"Oh, shit, baby, please…hold on," she yelled. He began to stroke her faster and she held on with all her might. As he stroked her, she began to get accustomed to the size of his dick and her pain became pleasure. "Umm, baby, that feels good," she moaned, pushing herself up on him so he could go deep.

He grabbed her by the legs and folded them together. He wrapped his right arm around her legs and leaned to the side so he could see her sex faces. He slid deep inside her, touching the back of her pussy. She bit down on her bottom lip and took everything he had to offer.

He held her tight as he thrusted in and out of her. "Oh, yes, my love…oh, yes." She was in pure ecstasy and didn't want this moment to end, she had waited what seemed like forever to give herself away and God knows it was worth every second.

He slowed down, feeling the perspiration dripping down his body. He pulled out of her and rolled her onto her stomach. He laid down on her and slid inside her from the back. He slow stroked her from behind. He gripped her dreads in his hand and whispered in her ear as he made love to her. "From the moment I met you I knew you would be mine. I love you so much. You are the air I breathe and without you there is no me. Umm…baby, I'm about to cum.

He could feel the sensation building up and wanted to meet her at the finish line. He lifted up and gripped her by the dreads and palmed her ass with the other hand. He thrusted inside her. He could feel her body beginning to tremble. "Oh, baby, oh, baby…I'm cumming."

Her body jerked uncontrollably. She buried her face in the mattress to muffle her moans. He was about to nut. His body trembled. He fucked her faster. "Oh, shit, baby, I'm 'bout to… oh shit…oh shit, I'm cumming, baby." She was having multiple orgasms. She came long and hard.

"Awww, fuck, baby." He exploded inside her. He wrapped her in his arms and held her until they fell into a deep sleep.

CHAPTER 45

After numerous attempts to contact her mother, Martinez put her phone back in her pocket. She got in her car and made a trip to Lopez's house. She took an alternate route where she would be there in 15 minutes. She had a bad feeling and for the life of her she couldn't shake the feeling. She felt bad about standing her mother up on their dinner date, but she was going to make it up to her and her sister Mylasha.

She pulled up in the driveway, parked, and got out. The grass had grown up and the porch light was on. She took out her key and was about to unlock the door when she noticed the front door was cracked open. She pushed the door open and stepped inside.

The air was still and the smell of something, maybe rotten fruit, invaded her nose. "Mom, are you home?" she called out for her mother. There was no reply. She searched through the house, and it was empty.

She pulled out her cell to call her aunt Koontz. Martinez began to get nervous. She called Koontz and waited for her to pick up. Koontz picked up on the second ring. "Hey, Alisha."

"Aunty, can you please come over to the house. Something ain't right. I just got to my mother's house and the door was open. The car is gone but I can feel something is wrong, aunty."

"Okay, I'm on my way, baby, just stay right there."

"Okay, see you when you get here." Martinez ended the call.

She sat down on the couch in the living room so she could gather her thoughts. Where did she go and what day did she leave? Mylasha had to be with her, so she had to go somewhere she felt comfortable to take Mylasha.

Something dawned on her at that moment. About four mornings ago she had Intelligent Home installed for her mother and sister because of the break-ins that were going on in their neighborhood. She pulled out her phone and logged into the Intelligent Home application so she could review the camera footage over the last week.

For the last two days there was no activity at the house. She kept rewinding the footage until the night that she was going to meet her mother for dinner. She stopped the rewind and hit play.

Her mother was going up the stairs and Mylasha was on her phone. Soon a pizza delivery guy showed up and Mylasha paid for the pizza. Martinez skipped past the irrelevant portion of the video and continued to see what was coming up next. She hit play and started the video again.

Her mother was leaving. Her mother peeked in to check on Mylasha. She went to the front door and left. She let the video continue to play. Where the hell was she going at that time in the morning? An image caught her eye and she focused on the video.

Someone was in the house. She zoomed in to see if she could see their face. The person had on a mask and gloves. Her heart started to race. The intruder headed up the stairs. Once he was upstairs, he stopped at Mylasha's door and waited. After awhile the intruder took a picture of Mylasha. What the fuck is going on? Why would they take a picture of her sister? This was diversity, obtuse.

Nothing happened for the next hour-and-a-half. The intruder just stood there patiently waiting. After another 20 minutes had passed the intruder answered his phone. After the intruder finished the call, he put the phone in his pocket and entered Mylasha's bedroom.

Martinez placed her hand over her mouth and watched in anticipation. The intruder walked over to Mylasha and stood over her. The intruder slid his hand under her head and with one quick motion snapped her neck.

"Oh, shit!" she screamed and dropped her phone. "Oh my God, what the fuck…Mylasha! No, no, no, not my sister!" She broke down and started crying.

The door opened and Koontz walked in. Martinez ran into her arms crying. "Baby, what's wrong?" Koontz asked. Martinez couldn't speak, she just trembled in Koontz's arms.

"Mylasha is dead, aunty. Dead!" The pain in her voice let Koontz know that what her niece was experiencing was atrocious. Who would want to bring malevolence to her family, especially something so indelible and impetuous? Koontz didn't feel the full magnitude of what was going on.

"I fucking knew something wasn't right. I could feel it in my soul, aunty," Martinez said, breaking her embrace. She wiped her eyes but still was an emotional wreck. She bent down and picked up her phone and rewound the footage back to where the intruder was standing over her sister Mylasha. She passed the phone to Koontz so she could see what happened to her sister.

Koontz took the phone and hit play. What she saw was enough to drop her to her knees. She couldn't believe what she just saw. If Mylasha was murdered in her own home, there was no telling what had happened to her sister Lopez, Koontz thought.

Koontz knew her sister better than anyone. She knew that her sister had some dark secrets, but none that would jeopardize her family's safety. This shit wasn't adding up, but one thing for sure, she was going to find out what happened to her sister and why Mylasha was killed.

If there wasn't but one person that could help her, she knew it would be the father of her children, Grey.

"Come on now, time is money, Mr. Jones and we don't have time to waste," BK Red said in her feminine voice. Don't let the softness of her voice fool you. Many had underestimated her and now they have the eternal smell of daisies. She held the car door for Mr. Jones to exit.

Jones got out of the car looking like he was prejudiced. Sumo stayed close up on him. Sumo knew that he was trained to maneuver in situations like this. Sumo pulled his strap and nudged it in Jones' side. "Let's go." BK Red shut the car door and followed behind Sumo and Jones as they made their way inside the house.

Once they were inside the house Sumo told BK Red to check the house to make sure it was empty. Sumo held close to Jones. Sumo could see Jones contemplating and strategizing. "Unless you want your brain all over that flat screen, I suggest you remain focused. Your son and girl are counting on you," Sumo said. Sumo wanted to plant a seed that would keep Jones' mind on his family while they collected the money and drugs, plus they needed Stanburg before they could move forward with their plans.

Once she searched the house top to bottom, she told Sumo the coast was clear. "Okay good, now let's start with the safe. Where is the safe and what's the combination," Sumo asked Jones.

"The safe is behind that fish tank." Jones pointed to the fish tank hoping that they would let him unlock the safe. Jones had a Sig 45 handgun laid on the back of the fish tank. Jones pulled away from Sumo. "I will open it for y'all," Jones said.

After he took a couple steps, Jones' intentions hit Sumo. Jones was eager to want to open the safe himself, plus he suggested it. Something wasn't right. "Hold on player, we got it. Don't want you to get no stupid ideas and make us have to kill you," Sumo said. Jones froze in his footsteps after Sumo put the gun back in his spine.

CHAPTER 46

"B K Red, move that fish tank away from the wall." The Sig 45 handgun fell off the fish tank and hit the floor. BK Red and Sumo looked at each other. This bitch-ass pig was really about to try some James Bond shit, Sumo thought.

Sumo hit Jones in the back of the head with his gun, dropping him to his knees. He cried out in pain. "Next time you try some shit like that you won't have to worry about experiencing pain 'cause you won't be here," Sumo spat, slapping him upside the head again and kicking him to the floor. "A'ight, y'all got it, man. The combination is 16, 13, 12, 5, 7.

BK Red put in the combination and the safe clicked. She opened the safe. "Now that's what I'm talking 'bout," referring to the stacks of hundred-dollar bills laid in rows inside the safe. "Go ahead and bag that shit up," Sumo said. "Now where is the work at?" Sumo asked while tapping Jones on top of his head with the pistol.

"It's in the attic," Jones replied. Sumo waited for BK Red to finish.

"We good, homie?" Sumo asked BK Red.

"Yeah, we good," she responded, coming back in the house after putting the money in the car. BK Red picked up the Sig 45. Damn, this bitch is nice.

"Hold this nigga while I go up in the attic to get the work."

"I got you, homie," she said, cocking the hammer back on the Sig. She aimed it at Jones' head and winked at him. Forty-five minutes later they had the money and the work.

Sumo pulled out his phone to call Lil Don. He picked up on the first ring. "What's good?"

"We got the money and the work."

"A'ight, now we got to get Stanburg's address."

"Shit, we here now, all we got to do is have him hit up Stanburg and tell him the work ain't right and have Stanburg come here and we can murc his ass here."

"Cool, but I still want his address, so get it out of Jones."

"Fo sho, I got you," Sumo said. Sumo ended the call.

"Okay, Mr. Jones, so far so good. You have stuck to your word, and we will stick to ours, but there is the last part of the negotiation, and that is Stanburg's address. There is nothing to think about, Stanburg has to be eliminated for both our benefits. For one, once Stanburg finds out that you don't have the bricks anymore, you are a dead man. Second, you are a sergeant, so you know once Sanburg is out of the picture someone will take his position and you will move up in rank. It's a win-win. Plus, you gonna need the money now that we have your stash."

Everything was making perfect sense to Jones and he decided to give up Stanburg's address. "7549 Timberland Drive. Now can you let me and my family go?" Jones requested.

"Not just yet. We need you to call him and get him over here and we will take care of the rest," Sumo said. Sumo could feel the blood pressure in his hand pulsing as he gripped the pistol. He was surgical with his weapon and was ready to leave Stanburg's ass smoking. The more Jones delayed his request the tighter his hand gripped the pistol with anticipation. Sensibilities were forbidden in the game of war and Jones was close to becoming a casualty.

"Tell Stanburg something is wrong with the dope, and you need him to check it out 'cause you think it's been stepped on too much, the dope ain't as potent as the last." Jones pulled out his phone to call Stanburg. Stanburg picked up immediately.

"I take it business is going along smoothly."

"That's what I'm calling about. People is complaining about our product. They saying it is weak. If we try to put this on the streets it's going to fuck up our clientele, especially the influential and pretentious."

"Yeah, I feel you because the last shipment that we received wasn't bad, but it was not in comparison."

"If you are not busy can you stop by real quick so you can take a look at it?"

"Yeah, I'm on your side of town. I can be there in about five to 10 minutes."

"Okay, I'm here in Waters Edge Apartments, 913."

"Okay, 913. Are you by yourself?"

"No, but I'll be here when you get here." Jones ended the call. "He is on his way. He said he will be here in five to 10 minutes," Jones said.

"Okay, cool, we about to be out. When he get here put a bullet in his head and we will tell you where to pick up your girl and kid." Sumo took Jones' phone and placed it on the couch and positioned it in the upright position facing the door. He activated FaceTime on the phones so he could watch Jones after him and BK Red left.

Sumo and BK Red exited the apartment. Before they left, Sumo turned around to address Jones as he stood in the doorway. "Handle your business and we will handle ours." Sumo looked at the apartment number. Eight-three-one, 831…he replayed the phone conversation over in his mind. Jones told Stanburg 913. Bitch a nigga, he alerted Stanburg by giving him a fake apartment number knowing he would suspect something wasn't right and Stanburg would be on alert when he showed up.

Sumo still had his pistol in his hand and Jones' eyes got big as golf balls when Sumo aimed it to his chest. "Get the fuck back in the crib, you fucking pig," Sumo spat. Jones put his hands up and eased back. "Yo BK Red, grab that nigga's phone." She quickly retrieved the phone off the couch. "See, the problem with y'all pigs is that y'all think y'all are smarter than everyone else. So, smart guy, tell me what's two plus three?" Sumo said.

Jones' lips trembled as he spoke, "Five."

"That's right!" Boom! Boom! Boom! Boom! Boom! "Bitch-ass pig, let's go," Sumo barked.

Sumo and BK Red ran out of the apartment. They jumped in the car. Sumo got behind the wheel while BK Red rode shotgun. He threw the car in reverse and backed out the driveway. A black Crown Vic came to a screeching halt, blocking them in.

Stanburg jumped out of the Crown Vic with his gun drawn. "Get the fuck out of the car," he screamed.

BK Red leaned out the window and gave Stanburg everything she had. Boom! Boom! Boom! She kept squeezing until no bullet was left in her chamber.

Stanburg took cover. Bullets bounced off his police car, glass from his windshield covered the ground. Sumo stamped the gas, ramming into the front of the Crown Vic. BK Red dropped her pistol and let loose with the Sig 45 she recovered from Jones. Boom! Boom! Boom!

Stanburg crawled towards the back of his car. He couldn't get a shot off. Sumo threw the car in drive and pulled off, just missing an oncoming car. He fishtailed down the street as BK Red kept bust-ing. He got the car under control. He looked in his rearview mirror to see if anyone was behind him. There wasn't. He came to the end of the neighborhood and merged into the traffic on Raeford Road.

"Yo, call Lil Don for me." BK Red pulled out her phone and made the call. Once Lil Don was on the line, she passed Sumo the phone. "Yo, shit didn't go as plan. That nigga Jones made the call to Stanburg but he tipped him off. We just got in a shootout in broad daylight. We got the money and the work. We need a quick place to hide, homie, 'cause the police gonna be up on this whip in a second.

"Where you at right now, homie?"

"Coming down Raeford Road by Bunce Road."

"A'ight, hold on for a second, let me get Sunkist on the phone I'm 'bout to three-way him now."

Sunkist picked up on the second ring. "Yo, what's good, homie? Capital Hz."

"Yo, Sunkist, we in a fucked-up situation right now and need a quick place to duck off. We on Raeford Road about to pass Bunce Road."

"A'ight, take the next right onto Bunce Road. Once you get on the bunce make a left onto Portsmount Drive."

"Okay, I see it coming up now. A'ight I just turned onto Portsmount."

"Go all the way to the end and pull in. Go to the door and ask for D.C. or Erica. Tell them I sent you. You can chill there until the heat cool down. Lil Don will meet you out there."

"A'ight, 30 love, homie." Sumo ended the call.

CHAPTER 47

Shaggy Sean was back on his feet. The six months he spent in the county jail had put a real dent in his pockets. He had to drop $15,000 on a lawyer and then another $7,500 to make bond. Ever since he'd been fucking with Killa shit been sweet. It was time to re-up and Killa's shit was going to voicemail. He tried Killa a few more times but got the same shit, his voicemail. Man, don't tell me this nigga on the run again. He sat in his Jeep Gladiator puffing on some weed.

Since Killa wasn't picking up he had time to play. He looked at his Seiko Presage watch and saw it was 4:30 in the afternoon. He decided to hit up Meme to see what she was getting into. Plus, she gave the best head on the westside. He tapped on the phone icon on his dash and called Meme. She picked up on the third ring.

"Well damn, it's gonna rain, you calling me."

"Stop the bullshit. You know I be out here chasing that bag."

"Speaking of bags, you still gonna get my hair done?"

"Yeah, after I come over there and fuck it up."

"Boy, you know you can't even handle this pussy. If it ain't 11 and thick I don't even want it."

"Shit, you need to find you a horse then 'cause I can't do shit for you."

"Oh my God boy, you are fucking stupid. See, that's why I fuck with you. You keep a smile on my face. I need the joy in my life, especially after everything I been through."

"Yo, I'm 'bout to come get you so be ready in about 15 minutes, a'ight?"

"Okay, I will be out front waiting on you."

"Peace." Shaggy Sean ended the call.

His stomach started to talk to him, letting him know he hadn't eaten shit all day, especially now that it was 4:45 in the afternoon. He decided to hit up Cook Out. Their food was delicious and they had hella drinks. Fifteen minutes later he was at the drive-through ordering a double burger tray with sides of fries and a grilled chicken wrap. He pulled up and paid for the food. He thought about ordering Meme something but even if she had her own plate, she would still eat off his plate.

He waited about a minute-and-a-half. This side of town was dead, even mundane, if you will. He was handed his food. This chick looks mighty familiar, he thought about the chick passing him his food. "Yo, where do I know you from?" he asked.

She scrutinized him and chuckled. "I'm Meme's friend Star. I had met you that night when shit jumped off at the Big Apple Club," Star said. "I wanted to holla at you but you pulled up on my homegirl Meme, so you know how the game go."

"What time you get off, 'cause I'm 'bout to pull up on Meme now. Shit, maybe we can all get into something," Shaggy Sean said.

"You sexy and all but it ain't even that type of party, player," Star said, knowing Shaggy Sean's motive was to try to fuck her and Meme. "I got to get back to work but it was nice seeing you again." She shut the drive-through window and Shaggy Sean pulled off.

He ate as he maneuvered through traffic on Owen Drive. He passed Cape Fear Hospital and kept straight. Every now and then he checked his rearview mirror to see if any cops were behind him or coming up in the other lane. Being a level six felon and riding with a pistol you had to be on your shit, plus he had just got out, so going back to jail wasn't an option.

Ten minutes later he was pulling into Stewart Creek Apartments. Meme was standing outside her apartment building. He pulled up and told her to get in. She opened the door and got in.

"What was you doing at the Peppermint Rabbit the other night?" she questioned Shaggy Sean. He had told her he had to make a couple plays so he slid off to holla at the Lil Snow Bunny Brittany from Blunt Street. Meme was patiently waiting on a response. She knew she had him cornered and was waiting for him to lie.

"Yeah, I pulled up at the Peppermint Rabbit to serve this lil' white girl some snow," Shaggy Sean said.

She let it go 'cause all Shay told her was that she had seen him at the club. "A'ight, you off the hook 'cause I can't prove shit, but I know you on some bullshit," she said.

"Don't start tripping, Meme," Shaggy Sean advised her. She was starting to get on his nerves. He played it cool though. "Why you be tripping when I'm out here getting this money but ain't got nothing to say when I'm spending it on you?"

She didn't have shit to say. Meme just turned her head and looked out the window. "But you ain't got nothing to say now. Matter a fact, get out," Shaggy Sean snapped.

"Baby, I'm sorry, it's just you are always gone, and I be lonely and want you here with me. Shit is so complicated for me right now," Meme said.

Shaggy Sean eased up knowing what had happened to her. He knew her emotions were all over the place. "It's cool, baby. Shit, I ain't tripping, shit been crazy for me too out here, especially trying to get back to where I was before I got locked up. I got to provide for you, my mom, and my grandma. Shit, it's been days I don't even see a penny of my money, but I make that shit work." Shaggy Sean was smart. He had plenty of money, but she wouldn't know it.

"Baby, let me take the stress away," Meme said. She leaned over the stick shift and unzipped his pants. She pulled his dick out of hiding and took him into her mouth. He leaned his head back against the seat. He placed a hand on top of her head and introduced her to the rhythm of his choice.

His phone rang. He picked it up. It was the Snow Bunny calling. "Damn, I need to take this call, but shit, fuck it, I'll pull up on her later on." He rejected the call and put his phone on silent. He could feel himself about to nut. This shit was feeling way too good. He wanted to enjoy the head game she was giving him.

"Hold on, baby." She sucked harder. "Oh shit…baby, hold on, I'm 'bout to nut." He tried to slide his dick out of her mouth, but she grabbed onto his waist and swallowed him whole. He couldn't help but to explode in her mouth. As his body jerked, she swallowed every drop of him.

Once he relaxed and the tension left his body, she let go of him and licked her lips. "Now can I get my hair did?" she said with a devilish smile.

"Shit, you can get your nails done too after that performance," Shaggy Sean said. He got himself together and pulled off. He dropped Meme off at Angela's Hair Salon. He gave her $200 and asked her what time did she want him to pick her up. She told him she was good, that her, Shay, and Star was going to the gun range when Star got off work. He gave her a kiss and was about to pull off when he noticed Beans and Boogie crossing the parking lot.

He had heard Boogie had won his appeal and was home, but he never had a chance to pull up on him. Beans was from the 704 but had come to the Ville to fuck with them on the guns. He pulled up on them and let down the window. "What's good, my nigga?" Shaggy Sean said.

Beans clutched his pistol by instinct, trying to see who was in the Jeep. "A motherfucker home, nigga," Boogie said.

"I heard you was out but shit, you good, my nigga?" Shaggy Sean asked Boogie.

"Man, trying to make it out here. Shit hard especially trying to get accustomed back to society after 22 years in the joint. A nigga could smell some pussy and bust a nut."

"Nigga, you a fool for that one, but here is five-hundred to help you get on your feet." Shaggy Sean peeled off the money from his bankroll and handed it to Boogie. At the sight of the money Beans' eyes lit up, but when Shaggy Sean laid the Uzi across his lap the fire in Beans' eyes dimmed. Shaggy Sean looked at Beans and smirked. A robber knew a robber. "Yo, keep y'all head up, players. I'm out." Shaggy Sean slid up the window and pulled off. He had unfinished business with the Snow Bunny.

CHAPTER 48

Tiny Diamond and Tiny Harlem had gotten Stanburg's address from Sumo. They had orders from Lil Don to kidnap Tiffany and Stanburg's daughter Lilly. They had been following Tiffany for the last two days. They finally got their chance to move in once Tiffany picked her daughter up from a soccer game at Jack Britt Middle School. They patiently waited in a white Kia K5 for Tiffany to pull out form the school.

Tiffany drove a silver BMW 228i Gran Coupe with little Lilly in the passenger seat. Tiffany turned onto Skibo Road and they pulled out behind her. Tiffany was heading home which was right around the corner. They stayed a car length behind her. Tiffany took a left and pulled into the back of Hollywood Heights.

They turned right behind her and hit the gas, speeding past her. They jumped in front of her and hit the brakes. Tiffany slammed on the brakes but ran into the back of the car. Tiffany looked over to check on her daughter. Once she saw Lilly was okay she took off her seatbelt and hopped out of the car.

Tiny Diamond and Tiny Harlem were crouched down in the seats. Tiny Harlem had adjusted the rearview mirror so he could see behind him.

"Look at my fucking car!" Tiffany screamed. Tiffany was now standing directly behind their car.

"Let's go!" Both men jumped out with their pistols drawn. "Fuck your car, bitch," Tiny Diamond spat, pointing the gun in her face.

"No! Don't kill me, my daughter is in the car," she pleaded.

"Bitch, tell us something we don't know. Now, shut the fuck up."

She began to cry. "Y'all guys are making a big mistake. My husband is the captain of the Fayetteville Police Department."

Tony Harlem slapped her in the face with his pistol as the getaway van was pulling up. "Let's go," Lil Weezy shouted. Tiny Diamond ran to the side of the BMW and snatched Lilly out of the passenger seat. Lil Weezy threw open the side door of the van and Tiny Harlem pushed Tiffany into the van. Tiny Diamond dragged Lilly to the van by her hair while she was kicking and screaming. He threw her in the van and shut the side door. He hopped in the passenger seat and slammed the door shut.

They left the stolen Kia K5 behind as they pulled off. Tiny Harlem tied Tiffany up first and searched her for a phone. She had a phone in her pocket. He took the phone out of her pocket and passed it to Tiny Diamond. Tiny Diamond tossed it out the window.

Tiny Harlem tied up Lilly and patted her down. He didn't find nothing on her. "When my daddy catches y'all he gonna take y'all to jail!" Lilly shouted. The men laughed at her.

"Guess what. When we catch your daddy, we gonna send him to hell," Lil Weezy said. She sat back down and shut up.

Lil Weezy made sure to stay just under the speed limit. He stopped at the light and waited patiently for it to change. Tiny Harlem called Lil Don. He picked up immediately. "What's good?"

"We on schedule, homie, and we on our way."

"A'ight cool, I'm at the spot now. Sunkist is going to meet us out there in the country."

"Facts!" Tiny Harlem hung up and slid his phone in his pocket. The light changed. Lil Weezy thought to himself that it would be faster if they hit Ramsey Street and took it all the way down. It would take them straight into Bunnlevel. Once his mind was made up he pulled off.

They drove in complete silence until they hit the Harnett County line. "Yo, we got to take this left coming up," Tiny Harlem told Lil Weezy.

"Yeah, I think you right, it should say Chapel Church Road," Lil Weezy said. As they came closer to their turn the sign to Chapel Church Road came into view. Lil Weezy made a left and continued on the route.

They passed a couple of houses along the way but for most of the way they only saw trees and dirt roads that extended to fields. "Man, where in the fuck this nigga got us going?" Tiny Diamond said.

"To the land of no return," Lil Weezy said as he drove.

They passed a trailer park and Lil Weezy knew his turn was coming up soon. He saw the dirt path coming up on his right. He slowed the van down and turned onto the dirt road. They could feel the bumps in the road and hear the rocks under the tires. There were trees on both sides of the road as tall as you could see.

They drove along the dirt road for approximately five minutes before they saw cars parked at the end of the road. Lil Weezy pulled up and parked. He cut the engine and everybody got out, leaving Tiffany and Lilly in the van. Tiny Harlem stood by the side of the van with the side door open so he could keep an eye on Tiffany and Lilly.

Lil Don and Sunkist walked up to the van and peaked in. "Get them out of the van," Sunkist said.

Lilly was the first to say something between her and her mother. "Why are you doing this to us?" Lilly spoke with complete innocence in her voice.

"People make bad choices in life and the one that they care about most is used as an avenue to get to them," Sunkist replied to Lilly's question.

Smooth picked Lilly up and placed her on his shoulders. "Take her over there and set her in one of those chairs."

The area where they are is surrounded by trees. There is a huge lake behind them and nothing else but field and dirt. Everybody parked in a circle. There were three chairs that sat in the middle of the circle. The chairs were for Tiffany, Lilly, and most of all Stanburg.

Smooth sat Lilly down in one of the chairs. He returned to the van and got Tiffany and stood over her. He pulled out a burner phone. "What is your husband's number?" Tiffany quickly spitout the digits 910-583-5515. Sunkist called the number. Stanburg picked up on the first ring.

"Hello! Who is this?"

"You been looking for me, now you have me. But question is, do you want to live or die for Tiffany and your daughter Lilly?"

"You son of a bitch, if you harm them, I will hunt you down and kill you myself."

"I see you done watched too many cop movies."

Tiny Harlem whispered in Sunkist's ear, "Father and Sandman just pulled up in front of his crib now."

"If you ever loved Tiffany or Lilly you will do exactly what I say. You will go outside and get in the car that's waiting for you now. If you choose not to you will never hear their voices again."

Sunkist held out the phone towards Tiffany and Lilly. "Daddy, please come get me, I'm scared." Sunkist put the phone back up to his ear.

"So, what's it going to be, captain? And believe me I will know if you try to alert your playmates. Thirty seconds, now choose."

"I'm walking out now."

Stanburg ended the call. Sunkist sat on the hood of his car and waited for Father and Sandman to pull up.

CHAPTER 49

Angel laid in blood in a Night End Hotel room. Blood ran from her mouth as she tried to speak. Star, Meme, and Shay stood over her body. "Damn, she looks fucked up," Star said. Meme and Shay stood in silence. Payback was a motherfucker and revenge was sweet. Revenge had an internal taste that lasted.

Star smiled devilishly, looking at her handy work. Star got Angel's phone and went through the contacts until she found Fire's number. Star called Fire. She picked up on the second ring.

"Damn, bitch, I didn't think you was ever going to call."

"Bitch, shut your simple-minded ass up. Who you thought this was? Angel? Nah, Angel's ass is laid out in the middle of this floor hanging on for her life, bitch. If you give a fuck about this bitch, she will be in room 212 at the Night End. Hope you make it on time," Star said.

"Bitch, you got all that mouth. Be there when I get there. I knew I should have killed y'all bitches when I had the chance, and you better pray to Jesus, Buddha, and Allah if she dies," Fire said.

"Don't play with me, play with your pussy." Star threw the phone by angel. Star, Meme, and Shay left the hotel room. Angel picked the phone up.

"Hello? Hello?" Fire asked.

"Them bit…ches…ju…jumped…me…Fire…"

"Hold on, Angel, I'm on my way. They said you was at the Night End. Is that the one on Bragg Boulevard?"

"Yes! Please hur…ry Fire, I'm scared."

"I'm on my way now." Fire hung up. She called Sunkist. He picked up immediately.

"What's up, baby?"

"Baby, something happen to Angel. Where you at?"

"I'm out here in the country about 35 minutes from the Ville."

"Okay, I'm 'bout to go get her, okay?"

"A'ight, but look, send me a picture of this chick before you leave. I know that's your bestie and all that, but I don't know her. You are my first priority, feel me?"

"Okay baby, I love you and I will see you at home." Fire ended the call.

Oh my God, let me send this boy this damn picture. She quickly went into her picture gallery and found a picture of her and Angel and sent it to Sunkist. She grabbed her keys and ran out the door. She jumped in her BMW M235i Gran Coupe and sped off. She left Southern Pines going 120 mph. She made it to the Ville in 30 minutes.

She pulled into the Night End Hotel and parked. She hopped out of her car breathless. A couple was coming out of a hotel room. She asked them where was room 212? They pointed to the upper level. She ran upstairs. Once she reached the top level, she looked left to right…210, 211…. She found room 212.

She ran over to the door and let herself in. She stepped in the room and saw Angel balled up on the floor. Blood was everywhere. "Oh my God, Angel, are you okay?" Angel just moaned. Fire went and bent down beside her. Angel had so much blood on her face she couldn't see where it was coming from. "Hold on, angel, I'm going to go in the bathroom and get some washcloths and a towel so I can get some of the blood off of you."

Fire ran in the bathroom and pulled a washcloth off the hook. She ran it under some warm water. She squeezed some of the water out of the rag to leave it damp. She grabbed a towel and exited the bathroom.

Fire couldn't believe her eyes. Angel had a pistol aimed at her chest. "Unique, don't move!" Angel shouted. Angel had the pistol on her and had her phone up to her ear. Angel told whoever was on the other end that they could come in now and she hung up the phone.

"Angel, what is going on? Please talk to me, I'm your fucking friend!" Fire screamed. Angel remained silent until the door opened.

Fire felt so stupid. She knew she had been setup. Fire began to tremble from anger and the betrayal of her childhood friend. "Bitch! That's how you going to do me? Me?! The only real bitch in your corner?" Fire began to cry knowing she would never be able to live the dream she so desperately wanted.

Grey stood in the doorway as officers surrounded her. They placed her in handcuffs and escorted her out of the hotel. Angel and Grey walked beside her.

"Great job, officer Martinez," Grey patted her on the back.

Fire looked at Angel. "Bitch, you a fucking cop?!" Fire spat.

"Officer Fisher, can you place her in the back of my car? I would like to interrogate her first," Grey said.

Officer Fisher gave Fire a devilish smile. "Sure thing, boss." Officer Fisher escorted Fire to Grey's personal car. Officer Fisher opened the back to the Land Rover and put Fire in the backseat. He made sure she was secured and stood by the back door until Grey got in the driver's seat. Officer Fisher closed the back door and walked off.

Grey locked the car doors and pulled off. "Ms. Unique Spellmen, I give you your props. You are one little hard bitch to find," Grey said as he drove. Y'all motherfuckers is going to learn it's only one king in this city and it's me."

"Man, don't nobody care about that Kings of New York speech shit you talk. Suck my dick, nigga!" Fire snapped, drops of spit flying from her lips. Fire was livid and at this point didn't give a fuck if she died. Life without Sunkist was a death sentence to her.

"I sure could use a bitch like you on my team, but I think I'll put you with the rest of your team in a box, bitch. Matter of fact let's see how much your nigga really love you. Your life for his."

CHAPTER 50

Trearina was coming out of Dollar General after buying her kids some snacks when police cars were pulling into the Night End. Something always jumps off over there. She decided to be nosey and went to see who the cops bagged this time. Whoever it was, there had to be a warrant for murder or they were pushing bricks the way they had the hotel blocked off. Is that Grey? She thought. For that nigga to be on the scene, this shit got to be big. Trearina put her stuff in the car and made her way across the street to the Night End. She pulled out her phone so she could get some pictures for her post on Facebook. Oh shit, they bringing them down now. Looks like a female.

The officers were bringing Fire down the steps. As she got closer, Trearina's heart began to race. No! No! No! Not Fire! Oh my God…what the fuck?! She bent down beside a car and peaked over the hood when the coast was clear. She held up her phone and took a couple of pictures. She brought the phone back down and took a look at the pictures she took. She just shook her head. Hold on, ain't that the chick Fire said she grow up with? She zoomed in on the picture. Hell yeah, that's her, but why would she be with Grey?

She had to put Sunkist on point. She tried to call Sunkist, but he wasn't picking up. She sent him a text and told him to call her. She ran back across the street and hopped in her car. She pulled up to turn onto Bragg Boulevard. She waited until Grey pulled out. She let a couple of cars get behind Grey and then she pulled out. She made sure to stay a couple of cars back. She didn't want to tip him off that he was being followed. She kept a low profile, moving with the traffic. They passed the jailhouse. What the fuck was Grey doing? Trearina thought. Once they passed the police department, she knew Grey was up to no good. She followed him into Hope Mills and wondered where he was going.

CHAPTER 51

The sun had gone down. Sunkist's phone had died, so he put it on the car charger. When he looked up he could see a set of car lights coming up the path. Once he saw the black Ford Focus, he knew that it was Father and Sandman.

The Ford Focus pulled up and parked. Father was the first one to exit from the passenger seat. Sandman cut the engine and stepped out. He closed the car door behind him and pulled his strap. He stood by the driver's side of the car and waited.

Father opened the back door to the car. "Get the fuck out, pussy," Father spat. Stanburg was handcuffed with his own handcuffs. Stanburg slid to the edge of the car seat and placed his feet on the ground. He stood up. Father escorted him to a chair that sat in front of his wife and kid.

Lilly saw her father and yelled out, "Daddy!" she jumped up and tried to run to her father but fell because her feet were tied. Sunkist's heart went out to Lilly because she didn't deserve this shit, but it is what it is.

Sunkist walked up to Stanburg. "Now, as you look at your wife and kid, ask yourself, was it worth it? Killing my people in the name of power and greed. Selling the same drugs we sell 'bout got a nerve to want to eliminate me and mine. It's enough of money out here for all of us. I'm going to ask you one more time, and if you lie, I'm going to set Tiffany on fire. Then if you lie again, I'm going to set Lilly on fire, and you can watch your little girl burn to death. Then I'ma put a bullet through you skull and me and my homie gonna leave this bitch. My first question, who is y'all plug?" Sunkist asked.

"You gonna kill us anyway if I tell you the truth or not," Stanburg said.

"Wrong answer." Sunkist went to his trunk and opened it. He pulled out two five-gallon jugs of gasoline. He placed the jugs on the ground and closed his trunk. This motherfucker think I'm playing with him. He picked up one jug and walked over to Tiffany and began pouring the gasoline over her head. She began to scream as the gas began to burn her eyes. She had a hard time breathing but managed to tell her husband he ain't shit. She couldn't run or escape. Smooth had tied her and Lilly to the chairs. She fell over in the chair, still cursing.

"You sorry son of a bitch. You gonna let them kill me while you sit there and don't say shit? I've been with you for 20 years, motherfuck-er. Twenty years and you will let me go out like this," she screamed.

Sunkist tossed the jug. He reached in his pocket and pulled out a lighter. Sunkist looked to Stanburg, giving him one last chance before he set his wife on fire. Stanburg remained silent and didn't utter a word. Sunkist tossed the burning lighter onto his wife, igniting her in flames.

The fire lit up the night as Tiffany's screams echoed through-out the pine trees. She twisted and kicked as the fire burned her alive. The smell of burning flesh filled the air as Tiffany's body came to a rest. The flames kept burning, turning her body into a crisp matter.

Lilly was traumatized. Her mouth was open, but nothing came out. She just stared into space.

"Now, I'm going to ask you that question again. Who is Grey's plug?" Sunkist asked Stanburg. Stanburg remained silent. "Fine with me." Sunkist walked over and picked up the second jug of gasoline. He walked over and lifted the jug and began pouring the gasoline in Lilly's lap.

"Daddy, no! Please help me! Please!" She began to cry and call for help. Once the bottom half of the little girl was covered in gasoline, Sunkist asked for a lighter. Father passed him his.

Sunkist struck the lighter, igniting the flame. He looked over towards Stanburg, giving him opportunity to come clean. Stanburg remained silent. Sunkist tossed the lighter back to Father and pulled his strap. "You got to be one bitch-ass motherfucker to hold a nigga's life higher than your daughter's, your own flesh and blood. Sunkist was pissed.

He walked up on Stanburg and shot him in the chest twice. Boom! Boom! Stanburg cried out in pain. "Shut your bitch-ass up." He hit him again. Boom! Knocking off his kneecap.

"Please, man! Oh God!" Stanburg cried.

"Fuck you! It was no please when your wife was calling out to you." He hit him again. Boom! The XD-40 was knocking chunks of flesh from his body. Boom! Boom! Boom! He hit him in both feet, knocking one of his shoes off.

"Man, it's the mayor, Mayor Peterson," Stanburg said.

Sunkist looked at Smooth. Then he searched the faces of the men that stood with him to make sure he heard Stanburg correctly. "The mayor," he repeated. This shit was all starting to make sense. The whole time Grey was just a pawn on the chessboard. It was the mayor that was funding everything. Grey was just the means to eliminate them.

"Where do the mayor stay?" Sunkist asked.

Stanburg said, "1129 Madison Drive in Hope Mills."

Sunkist walked over and picked up the jug of gasoline and poured it all over Stanburg. "Yo, Father, set that bitch on fire so we can get the fuck out of here."

Father tossed the lighter onto Stanburg. He began to scream but his screams fell on deaf ears.

Sunkist walked behind Lilly and hugged her, telling her he was sorry for what she had to witness, and he apologized for the cards she was dealt. He kissed her on top of her head then took a step back and pulled the trigger. Boom! Her body slowly leaned over. A tear slid from the corner of his eye for the life he just took. He saluted his homies, hopped in his car, and headed home.

CHAPTER 52

It was 6:15 in the afternoon and Koontz was ready to go home. It had been a long day, but she had a mission to complete. She wished she had never opened that letter and now she saw why it was for Sunkist's eyes only.

Her curiosity was killing her, plus she wondered if anything in that letter would give a hint or clue on her sister's whereabouts. She turned in her equipment and said her goodbyes to a few officers on her way out the door. She exited the building feeling the minimal breeze of the summer wind. She felt overwhelmed and the weight of the world's extreme pressures seemed to weigh on her shoulders.

She took a deep breath and exhaled, trying to calm her nerves. She crossed the parking lot. Her ultimate goal was she had to get Martinez and Sunkist in the same room without Sunkist killing both of them. She became frantically nervous, and an unpleasant feeling rested in her fingertips. Get it together, Koontz, she whispered to herself before opening the car door.

She got in and closed her car door. She put on her seatbelt, checked her mirrors, and hit the ignition. She turned the radio on so she could hear the afternoon mix on Foxy 99.1. She put the car in reverse and backed up. She cut on her A/C and pulled off. She pulled out her phone and called Sunkist. He picked up on the second ring.

"Long time, no hear."

"I'm sorry, I've been busy, and the new assistant district attorney is a pain in my ass. She think she can save the world in a day. But anyways, I need to talk to you. It is very important."

"You know shit is crazy right now and you been M.I.A. Now you call talking 'bout you need to talk to me. How I know this call ain't being trace right now?"

"Oh, for real, that's how you coming at me?"

"I know where your loyalty lay, Koontz, and it's not with me."

"I can see why you said that, but I have never betrayed you and I would never dishonor my sister by turning you in or trying to set you up. You know this. There is something Lopez wanted you to know. She mailed me a letter and told me to make sure I give it to you. I'm not going to lie, I did read it and the information in that lett…well, I think it will be best for you to read it for yourself. Is there a place we can meet?"

"A'ight, you can meet me tonight, 10 p.m. on Cliffdale behind the Cook Out. There is a dead-end street, one way in. I put this on my life, if you are playing games, you will be on the morning news." Sunkist ended the call.

Koontz looked at the screen on her phone which read "Disconnected." She sat her phone on the passenger seat and turned into her neighborhood. There were a couple of kids playing basketball in the middle of the street. She slowed down and beeped her horn so the kids would get out of the street. "Hey, Ms. Koontz," one of the kids said, waving to her as she passed. She threw up her hand in acknowledgement. Two minutes later she was pulling up in her driveway. She parked and cut the engine. She grabbed her purse, threw her phone in her purse, and got out of the car, closing the door behind her.

The front door to her house was open. Mikyla and Talila must already be home. She looked over to the side street and saw a black Land Rover Defender. She knew that car from somewhere and knew her baby father Grey had stopped by to see his daughters. "The day just couldn't get no better," she sarcastically said. She reluctantly wanted to get back in her car but she needed to talk to him. She made her way in the house.

Mikyla met her at the front door, running into her arms. "Mommy, mommy," Mikyla yelled. Mikyla wrapped her arms around her mother, happy to see her. Koontz bent down and kissed her on her forehead.

Talila was sitting on the living room sectional beside her father. It's a damn shame how much Talila looked like her father, Koontz thought.

Grey got up and gave Koontz a hug and kiss on the cheek. "How was your day?" Grey asked.

"It was hard, but I got through it. Can we talk for a second? I need to ask you something," Koontz said.

"Sure! Let's go upstairs," Grey suggested. They politely dismissed the children and made their way upstairs. They went into the bedroom and sat on the edge of the bed.

"First off, how have you been?" Koontz asked.

"Another day, another dollar," he replied.

Koontz began to strip out of her work clothes as she talked. "So, I wanted to ask you when was the last time you seen Lopez 'cause I been calling her and she ain't picking her phone up. I went by her house today and she wasn't there. I went inside her house and the house smelled like nobody has been there in days."

Grey was zoomed in on the apple shape of her ass, but the mention of her sister's name snapped him out of his daze. "I haven't heard from her. Last time I seen her she was leaving work on her way home, I think," Grey said. "I hope everything is okay with her, but I will have someone check on it for you."

"Thanks so much," she said.

Grey stood up and walked up on Koontz. He put his arms around her and palmed her ass. She broke his embrace. She had just got off work. "That's all y'all niggas think about is pussy. I just told you I'm worried about my sister and I'm not in the mood for the bullshit right now. I'm 'bout to take a shower. I will talk to you later," she said. She went into the bathroom and slammed the door.

Grey knew he had fucked up and getting some pussy was out the window. He went back downstairs, kissed both his daughters goodbye, and left.

Koontz took a long shower to relax her body. She needed a stress reliever. She cognitated pensively as the water cascaded down her body. She was in the middle of a hostile situation between adversaries and enemies. She was playing a dangerous game. If Grey found out that she was in contact with Sunkist she would be nonexistent.

She cut the water off. She put both hands on the shower wall and lowered her head. This shit has to end. The thought of her continuing to do business with Sunkist would end tonight. She didn't want to straddle the fence any longer, it was exasperating. She would do him this last favor on the strength of her sister, but after this she would cut all ties.

She stepped out of the shower and grabbed a bath towel and dried off. She got dressed and went downstairs. She picked up her purse and got her phone. She called Martinez. Martinez picked up on the third ring.

"Hey, aunty."

"I need you to come to my house now, we need to talk."

"Okay, but is everything okay?"

"I will let you know what's up when you get here."

"Okay, I'm on my way now."

Koontz hung up the phone. She sat down on the couch. Mikyla came and sat in her lap. She hugged her little girl knowing the move she was about to make could be her last. She rested her head on the back of the couch and waited for her niece to arrive.

Forty-five minutes later she heard a car pulling in her driveway. Mikyla had fallen asleep in her arms. She slid from under her daughter and stood so she could open the door for Martinez.

She opened the door and Martinez came inside. Martinez hugged her aunt and sat down on the sectional couch. "So, what is this all about, aunty?"

"I'm going to need you to trust me and just take a ride with me around 9:45 tonight."

Martinez looked at her watch, it read 8:55 p.m. "Aunty, you are making me nervous. Can you just tell me what is going on?" Martinez said, struggling to keep her temper in check.

"Baby, if it was that easy, best believe me I would, but it's not, so I need you to trust me."

"Okay. You have always had my back when I needed you, so I will do as you ask of me, but I'm telling you, I don't like being in the blind."

"You know I will never let anything happen to you," Koontz said.

"I know, aunty, it's just the unknown is what scares me.

"Let me ask you something since this is our first time sitting down talking in awhile. I noticed every time I go over to the police department to speak with detectives or retrieve evidence you have not been in the office once. Plus, after I got you the job, I told Grey to keep me informed on your progress, but he hasn't told me nothing, and that's not like him, especially him knowing you are my niece."

"Well, to be honest—and I mean it, aunty, this stays between us—when I got the job Grey immediately took me under his wing and assigned me to an undercover operation called Black Ops. I did my field training and once I was finished, I was given a list of names and was told to track them down and report only to Grey or Stanburg. I started my investigation. One by one I came across the members of a lethal criminal organization that I was assigned to take down by Grey. So far, I have did my job to the best of my ability. I only have one more member to track and Grey will give me a recommendation so I can become a federal agent."

"That sneaky son of a bitch, I knew something wasn't right." Koontz began to pace the floor. "Listen to me and listen to me good, you are in way over your head. The people you are tracking will kill you, me, and everybody we love if they find out who you are," Koontz said.

"I know how dangerous it is, aunty, that's why I'm never around the police station. I only report to Grey and Stanburg, but now that Stanburg is dead I only report to Grey."

"That motherfucker is playing you to get what he wants and that is to take over the streets. He is using you to hand it over to him on a silver platter."

"What are you telling me, Grey is dirty?" Martinez questioned.

"Little girl, you better open your pretty little eyes and see what is going on around you."

Martinez didn't know what to believe. She was lost and looking for answers to a puzzle that lay disconnected. She thought she was just doing her job, but the whole time she was a puppet being strung along by Grey. She had just turned Fire over to Grey and now another piece was removed from the game. Sunkist was the checkmate.

Koontz looked at her watch—9:40 p.m. "It's time to go." She ran upstairs and got the letter that Lopez wrote her sister. She got the letter and made her way downstairs. "Talila, watch your sister, I will be back in a little bit." Koontz and Martinez got in the car and pulled off.

Sunkist sat on the hood of his Alfa Romeo. He checked his watch, it was 10:01 p.m. He took a look around to check his surroundings. Father and Sandman were at their posts behind a big oak tree. Smooth and Lil Weezy sat on the porch of an abandoned house. Tiny Harlem and Tiny Diamond posted up at the back of the Cook Out. Sumo and BK Red were in their cars parked at the beginning of the street. Lil Don sat on his trunk holding an AR-15 with a drum on it. He looked at his watch again—10:11 p.m. Man, fuck this shit! Sunkist thought and was about to get in his car and leave when a set of car lights caught his attention.

A Hyundai Sonata turned onto the street. Sunkist stood up and waited for the car to pull up. Koontz parked the car, turned off the lights, and cut the engine. She got out of the car first, then Martinez got out. Martinez stayed close to her aunt.

They walked up to Sunkist. Martinez began to tremble once she recognized who she was now standing in front of. She looked over towards her aunt and wondered why the fuck her aunt would put her in a fucked-up predicament.

He pulled his phone out of his pocket. It was Trearina so he answered. "Yo, shit is real right now, they got Fire, I'm following Grey now…I'm about to send you some pictures."

"Your phone is breaking up. What did you say about Fire? Hello…hello? Trearina!" The call disconnected. He looked at the screen and saw the call had dropped. He tried to call her back, but her phone went straight to voicemail. Seconds later he received a text from her: I'm sending the pictures now. He slid his phone in his pocket.

"What's up? What is so important that it couldn't been said over the phone?" Sunkist asked.

"My sister mailed me a letter and told me to give it to you. Before you read this letter, I want you to know I had no clue or knowledge about this," Koontz said. She reached in her pocket and pulled out the letter and handed it to Sunkist.

He took the letter out of the envelope. His phone alerted him that he had a text message. He pulled out his phone and checked the message. What he saw made his heart drop. They had Fire. His soul felt like it left his body as he stared at his screen. He slid to the next picture. He looked up at Martinez and back at his phone. His blood began to boil with hate. He went to his gallery to make sure he wasn't tripping. He looked for the picture Fire sent him earlier of them. He found the picture and indeed it was her.

"Yo Lil Don, come here for a sec," Sunkist said.

Lil Don hopped off the trunk. "What's good, homie?"

"Hold my phone for me." Sunkist passed his phone to Lil Don. He reached in his waist and pulled out his XD-40 handgun and put it to Martinez's head. "Bitch, you set Fire up?" Sunkist spat.

Martinez couldn't speak. She was dead wrong and her disloyalty would cost her her life.

"Please don't kill her, Sunkist," Koontz cried. "She is lost and didn't know she was being played."

"Give me one reason why I shouldn't blow this bitch's brains all over this pavement," Sunkist shouted, about to pull the trigger.

"Because she is your daughter."

Sunkist looked at Koontz for confirmation. "What the fuck you talking 'bout?" Sunkist spat.

"Read the letter. Just read the letter," Koontz cried.

Martinez didn't know what to think. Everything seemed to start moving in slow motion. Sunkist passed Lil Don his pistol. Sunkist unfolded the letter and began to read:

"I want to start off by saying I never stop loving you. Even though our paths lead to our separation you remain in my heart. When I was younger I dreamed of us getting married, buying a big house, and having kids. When I got pregnant I had to make a choice, not for me but for the future of our baby. Knowing the lifestyle you live would never lead her to a righteous path that would provide her with freedom and longevity of a life without death, pain, and destruction, I chose to tell you I had a abortion to keep our child safe. I have nothing but love and respect for you so I decided to tell you the truth hoping she is enough to make you change your perspective because she needs you. Love you always, Lopez."

Sunkist knew Lopez wrote the letter. Sunkist looked over at his daughter. He passed her the letter and let her read it. After she finished, he gave her some time to process it.

"Daddy, I'm sorry," she lowered her head.

Sunkist walked over to Martinez. He put his hand under her chin and lifted her head up. "You got my blood in you. Don't ever lower yourself in front of nobody. Keep your head up so you can see the world for what it is." He gave his daughter and hug and kissed her on the cheek. Blood is thicker than water.

"Okay Koontz, let me show you something." He got his phone from Lil Don and pulled up the pictures and texts that Lopez sent him the night she went missing. "Okay, Lopez sent me these pictures. She wanted me to know her whereabouts if something happen to her."

Koontz looked at the pictures and noticed the picture of Grey hanging on the wall. She was in his home. "When I asked him the other day when was the last time he seen her he said leaving work," Koontz said.

"Daddy, look at this." Martinez showed Sunkist the video of Mylasha being murdered.

"That motherfucker in that video is Stanburg. Grey must tried to use Lopez to get at me but she refuse to cooperate so he killed her," Sunkist said. Sunkist's phone rang. He looked at the screen, it was Trearina. He answered the call. "What's up, Tee?"

"I followed Grey all the way to the mayor's mansion in Hope Mills. Grey took Fire inside, but I can't see shit else. There is a lot of guards surrounding the mansion."

"We on our way." Sunkist ended the call. "Let's go," Sunkist shouted. "Martinez, come ride with me." Sunkist and Martinez hopped in the Alfa Romeo and Sunkist pulled off. Everyone else fell in line.

Twenty minutes later they were pulling up to a stash house that held the organization's firearms. Sunkist hopped out of his car, leaving it running. Everyone else parked and stood by their cars.

Sunkist unlocked the stash house. He pushed the door open and stepped inside. He cut on the lights and made his way to the kitchen. He slid the kitchen table aside, bent down, and started to remove the kitchen tile from the floor. Once the tile was removed, he pulled on the trap door until it gave. He ran back to the front door and motioned for everyone to come in. He went back in the kitchen and climbed down the ladder into a hidden part of the house.

Once he was in the gun room he cut on the light, illuminating the gun room. Smooth and Lil Weezy climbed down into the gun room. There were glass cases filled with guns and chests that held the ammo. One by one they all climbed down into the gun room.

"Strap up," Sunkist ordered. Each man and woman picked the weapons of their choice. Sunkist opened one of the glass cases and pulled out a street sweeper, all black with the pistol grip handle.

Martinez stood beside her father. She picked up a chrome-plated German Tec-9. She slid the clip out and pulled the hammer. "Nice!" she said.

Koontz chose a baby AK-47 with the woodgrain stock.

BK Red opened one of the glass cases. There were two twin fully automatic Smith & Wesson 45s sitting on the shelf. She picked up both of them and felt the weight of them. They were light. She smiled. "These bitches is mine."

Once BK Red left the case, Smooth stepped up and eagerly retrieved two Russian Uzis with extended stocks.

Lil Don's eyes lit up when he saw the rocket launcher. He ran over and snatched it off the wall. He tossed the strap over his shoulder. "I'm ready for war. Who ready? There will be no discrepancies with this bitch, I guarantee it," Lil Don said, holding the rocket launcher up like he was about to star in a Rambo movie.

Tiny Diamond's eyes rested on a 1911-A1 Springfield. He picked the gun up and kissed the barrel. One word came to his mind—malevolent.

Lil Weezy opted for the Glock 23.

Father was surgical with the 12 gauge.

"Yo, I got to have these," Sumo said, picking up two gold-plated XDS-40s.

Sandman scrutinized a MAK-90. It was camouflage with a black strap. He chose the powerful weapon with certainty.

Sunkist's phone rang. It was from a blocked number. He looked at the phone for a second. This could be about Fire, he thought. He took a deep breath and answered the call. "Speak!"

"You got two options. You can let this bitch die or you can give your life for hers. The choice is yours, but to be honest, I would love to put a bullet between her pretty little eyes. So, what are you going to do?"

"Yo, let her go and you can have the city. On my word we will leave the city and you will never hear from us again. I got 2.5 million I will give you as a sign-on bonus to accept my offer."

"You are missing the point of all this. My higher ups want your head. This is not about revenge. I got my revenge when I fucked your sweet bitch Lopez then broke that bitch's neck. So, no, there is no price tag you can put on this. The deal is your life for hers."

"I tried to be colloquial and come to an understanding with you, but we can get gangsta if that's how you want to go about it."

"Choose!" Grey shouted.

Sunkist hung up in his face. Sunkist looked around the room. "Listen up! The Ops got one of ours. If we got to take 100 of theirs, so be it. Tonight we live as one, we die as one. These are the moments that separate the real from the fake. Salute! Now, let's handle our business with these government police."

CHAPTER 53

Fire sat tied to a steel chair. She was naked and cold. The room she was in had no heat. She could hear the wind whistling above her head. She was without water and was thirsty. As she sat in the chair she tried to see through the darkness.

The room was pitch black. There were no windows in the room, just four walls and a door. The floor was made of concrete. She could feel the texture of the floor with her bare feet. How did this shit happen? She would never have seen it coming, not from Angel. Sunkist was right. She was glad she did send that picture to him. He knew she was the last person she was with. Maybe it would lead him to something.

She thought about the love they made. The way he held her. She didn't want to go out like this, vulnerable and weak. She was a soldier. Sunkist and Zionna instilled that mentality in her. She was built to sustain the adversity. She would not give these motherfuckers the satisfaction to see her weak. She had to embrace her storm and welcome it with open arms. If tonight was the night God called her home, then there was no negotiating shit, especially with this pussy-ass nigga Grey.

She heard the door being unlocked. She held her breath with anticipation. The door opened and she could see two figures enter the room. The light came on. Fire had to squint her eyes to see. As her focus cleared, she noticed one of the men was Grey. Who the fuck was the other guy? she thought.

"Ms. Spellmen, AKA Fire. My name, of course, is Mayor James Peterson. You don't know me, but I have been around for a long time. I helped build this city, me and my family, brick by brick. All that has transpired between us and y'all organization wasn't by chance or prediction. It was a path your sister Zionna chose for y'all. I loved Zionna with my heart and soul. I gave her my soul, my love, and respect. Then I trained her and molded her to run this city and then I gave her the red carpet to being the most powerful woman on the east coast. And what does she do? Betray me. That bitch stole $10 million from me and 500 bricks of cocaine. That money and my drugs formed the organization y'all are a part of today."

"My motive here is not to bring you harm, Ms. Spellmen, but business is business. Over the years I tried to reason with your sister, even after her disloyal ass stole my shit. I let her create and establish herself by her own free will and by her own means. Once she had established herself, I gave her one last chance to return what she took. You know what the bitch told me? She told me I'd have a better chance cumming in my hand than coming for her. So here we are."

Grey stood in silence.

"Now, there is a way out of this for you, Ms. Spellmen, but your life lays in the hands of your man." Fire listened intently, hanging on to every word Peterson said. "I have given your man an alternative. He can let you die here tonight, or he can give his life for yours. So, in order to catch your sister, I will eliminate her foundation so she can't stand."

Grey took the floor. "I contacted your sweet Sunkist and gave him the alternative and he hung up in my face. Big mistake."

Grey reached in his pocket and pulled out a six-inch blade. He walked over to Fire and stood behind her. Grey placed the tip of the knife in her side under her right arm. He leaned down until he was ear level to her and whispered in her ear. "Your team is locked away. Your man has disowned you and no one is coming to save you. I enjoyed killing Lopez. Stanburg killed Pressure and Killa. Soon we will have your sister's head on a stake as well, but you won't be around to see it."

He slid the knife deep inside her, puncturing her lung. She couldn't help but to cry out in pain. He pulled the knife out. Blood began to run down her side. Her shirt was turning bloody red. The scent of blood lingered in the air. Grey smiled to himself, enjoying the sound of Fire's pain.

"Y'all motherfuckers can kill me but my husband will not stop until both of y'all lay right beside me," Fire spat, spitting up blood. She was having a hard time breathing. The sweat dripped from her nose.

"You got a lot of mouth, bitch," Grey said while placing the tip of the knife under her other arm. "See, the problem with… what the fuck was that?!"

CHAPTER 54

Sunkist called Trearina. She picked up immediately. "I've been waiting for you to call. I'm still here, about 20 yards outside the gate."

"We about to pull up now. I'm driving through the gate. Hopefully we will have the best leverage and the element of surprise in our favor. Can you count how many guards there is?"

"There is three on the upper-level balcony and four on each corner of the mansion. You got two at the front gate and four inside."

"So, about a total of 12. We got to get in and get out before they call for backup. Yo, if this shit go sideways I want you to know you are appreciated. I love you. Sunkist hung up the phone and hit the gas.

The mansion's gate was about 10 yards away. "Hold on," Sunkist told Martinez as the car sped toward the front gate. The two guards stood on both sides of the gate. Sunkist rammed through the gate, destroying the front fenders and damaging the radiator. Smoke shot from the engine and water from the radiator covered the windshield, making it hard to see.

He kept his foot on the accelerator. He could hear gunshots and heard a bullet hitting the car. He could see the front steps that led to the front door of the mansion. Fuck it! He stomped the gas all the way to the floor. The car hit the steps and hydroplaned in the air, crashing through the front door.

The air bags shot out just in time, stopping Martinez's head from colliding with the dashboard. Sunkist blacked out and laid unconscious behind the wheel. Martinez shook him violently until he gained consciousness.

She had to momentarily abandon her father. She picked up the TEC-9 and tried to open the door. The passenger side door was jammed shut. Boom! Boom! Boom! They were taking on fire. She peaked over the dash and saw two guards. She slung the TEC-9 out the window and pulled the trigger. Tat! Tat! Tat! As the TEC-9 jerked in her hand she lifted herself up and slid out the window. She threw the TEC-9 in the motion of a Nike check before she hit the ground.

The first seven bullets ripped through the first guard's chest. The next three bullets hit the second guard in the face, killing him instantly. She got to her feet and ran around to the driver's side door and snatched it open. She helped her father get out of the car. Sunkist's vision started to come back. "You okay?" she asked.

"Yeah, I'm good."

There were gunshots and bullets flying everywhere outside of the mansion. They had to be careful not to get caught in the crossfire. Sunkist reached in the car and retrieved the street sweeper.

Koontz and Lil Don ran up the steps and into the mansion. "Y'all good?" Lil Don asked, almost out of breath.

"Yeah, we good over here," Sunkist said.

The gunshots came to a stop. Blood covered the front lawn and driveway. The guards were laid out across the establishment. "There are still a couple of guards left on the upper level," Sunkist said. "Smooth, Lil Don, and BK Red take the left wing. Tiny Harlem, Tiny Diamond, and Lil Weezy take the right wing. Father, Sandman, and Sumo handle the upper level. Fire is in this bitch somewhere," Sunkist said. "Now, let's bring her home."

Everyone dispersed. Sunkist paid attention to how the mansion was built. He looked at the walls to see how they were constructed. Nothing seemed out of place. The living room was huge. "See if y'all can find a door that leads to the bottom level of the house," Sunkist said.

They went their separate ways. Sunkist heard gunshots coming from the upper level. He checked the bookshelf to see if there was a trap door. There wasn't. he went into an office at the beginning of the left wing. "I found it," Martinez shouted.

Koontz and Sunkist came running. "Where are you at?" Sunkist asked, now standing beside Koontz.

"I'm in here," Martinez shouted from behind the fake fireplace. Martinez opened the fireplace that was mounted to a hidden door.

"How the fuck you find this shit?" Sunkist asked.

"All real fireplaces has a chimney or draft so the smoke can escape. This one doesn't have one, so I knew it was fake. I pulled on the handle and the door clicked."

There was a long, dark hall that led to a door at the end. Sunkist could see light coming from under the door. "She got to be in there," he said.

Smooth, Lil Don, and BK Red walked up behind Sunkist. "We searched everywhere."

"We did too," Tiny Diamond, Tiny Harlem, and Lil Weezy entered the room. Father, Sandman, and Sumo came in seconds later.

Sunkist spoke up. "There is a door at the end of this passage. If y'all searched the whole mansion and didn't find her or any sign of Grey and the mayor, then that is the only spot left." Sunkist gripped the Street Sweeper and lead the way down the hall.

Once he got to the door, he turned the knob. The door was unlocked. Sunkist could hear sirens in the distance and knew the cops were on the way. He took a deep breath and pushed the door open a little. He held the Street Sweeper chest level and took the barrel and pushed the door completely open.

Sunkist stepped into the room. Martinez and Koontz followed closely behind. Grey was standing behind Fire with a nine-millimeter handgun pressed to her head. Sunkist could see the blood stain on her shirt and knew she was hurt and needed medical attention. Sunkist kept the Street Sweeper aimed at Grey's chest.

"Nice for y'all to join us," Peterson said, getting out of his chair. Martinez and Koontz kept their guns on Peterson. "Little Ms. Martinez, you can kiss your job goodbye and rot in a prison cell with the rest of these motherfuckers," Peterson shouted. "This mansion is surrounded by cops. Yes, motherfuckers, the boys in blue. What y'all think, you was just going to walk up in here and…." Boom! Koontz shot him in the face, putting his brains all over the floor.

Sunkist moved closer to Fire but kept the Street Sweeper locked on Grey.

"Don't take another step, motherfucker. I will kill this bitch where she sits," Grey spat. Grey knew there was no way out of this. They weren't going to jail and there was no way he was going to leave this room alive.

"You know what? I done lived my life," Grey said, angrily pressing the gun harder against Fire's head. Fire's eyes were barely open. "Y'all can suck my dick. I will see y'all in hell but I'm taking this bitch with me." Grey gripped the pistol and pulled the trigger, click. Boom! Boom! Boom! Sunkist hit Grey in the chest with the first shot, lifting him off his feet. The other two shots hit the wall.

Martinez walked up on him and stood over him. "This is for my mother, motherfucker." Boom! She shot him between the eyes, ending his life.

Sunkist ran to Fire's aid. He untied her, picked her up, and carried her out of the mansion.

"Freeze! Put y'all hands in the air, now!" a police officer yelled over a loudspeaker.

Everyone frozen except Martinez and Koontz. Martinez flashed her badge and Koontz announced she was the head district attorney. The police lowered their weapons. "We need an ambulance immediately," Martinez ordered, "and let these people through so they can go home." Martinez stood with a couple of officers to inform them on what took place.

Ten minutes later an ambulance was pulling up. They put Fire on a stretcher and loaded her in the ambulance. Sunkist and Koontz rode with her to the hospital. Once at Cape Fear Hospital Fire was immediately taken into surgery. During her surgery Koontz left for a couple of hours then returned with Martinez. Sunkist was still sitting in the waiting room waiting on some type of report, anything, to let him know that Fire was okay.

Koontz and Martinez came over smiling and sat down beside him. He looked at Koontz and over to Martinez. "What the hell y'all two up to?" Sunkist asked the ladies.

"It's a surprise, daddy. You gonna have to wait to find out," Martinez giggled. Sunkist just shook his head.

"With y'all two it ain't no telling what to expect." Sunkist laid his head back against the wall and closed his eyes.

Three hours later a nurse woke him and told him that Ms. Spellmen's surgery was complete and that she was going to make it. She'd lost a lot of blood and is very weak, so they are not letting visitors see her until she gets better. He thanked her for the information.

"Well, let's go home and get some rest, and I see y'all back here tomorrow," Sunkist said. He hugged his daughter and gave her a kiss. He leaned over and kissed Koontz on the cheek. "Thanks for everything, and believe me, I know how hard it is for you right now, but we are family now and we will overcome this shit together."

Sunkist called Trearina to come pick him up. She was there within 15 minutes. She took him home and dropped him off. Sunkist went inside the mansion, took a shower, and went straight to bed.

The next day at 2:30 p.m. Sunkist woke from his sleep. He took a shower, did his hygiene, and got dressed. He jumped in his car and was at the hospital in 20 minutes. He walked to the front desk and asked the nurse if Unique Spellmen was allowed visitation today.

The nurse looked up her name. "Yes! She was just approved a couple hours ago," the nurse said.

"Thank you," he said and made his way to the hospital gift store so he could get her some flowers and balloons. After purchasing the items, he went back to the front desk to ask the nurse what room Unique Spellmen was in. After a few seconds she told him room 217. He thanked her once again.

He got to Fire's room and stopped. He inhaled deeply, letting the stress compress, and then he exhaled, letting the stress flow from his body. He opened the door and stepped inside. Fire's face lit up when she saw him. "Hey baby," she said.

Sunkist sat her flowers on the table beside her bed and tied her balloons to her bedrail. He leaned over and kissed her on the forehead. "Hey to you. How you feeling?" he asked.

"I'm good, still got a sharp pain in my side." As she spoke the door opened. Koontz and Martinez entered the room. Fire's eyes zeroed in on Angel. "Bitch, if I could get out this bed I would break your fucking neck," Fire spat.

Sunkist reached and took Fire's hand. "Baby, you got to let that shit go," he said.

Fire's eyes shot open so fast. "Nigga, what the fuck you mean?" she said, snatching her hand away from his.

"There has been alot of secrets, heartbreaks, and disloyalty in the path that we chose. I'm wiping my slate clean. I'm done with the streets and the dope game. I just want to be a loving and supportive husband that provides and gives you stability. I want to be a father and give my daughter something that I never had, which is peace." He put his arm around Martinez's neck.

Fire looked at Martinez and then at Sunkist. She could see the resemblance. What the fuck could possibly be next, Fire thought. Sunkist could see the steam coming off her head. She was not feeling this shit. "Fire, she is trying her hardest to right her wrongs. She stood with us and went to war for you. She is the reason we are standing here today and not in a jail cell."

Fire didn't like this shit, but she had to respect it.

"I'm sorry, Fire," Martinez said. Fire shot her a look. Boy, if looks could kill she would be D.O.A.

"Ummm…give her some time," Sunkist told Martinez, moving her out of Fire's reaching distance. "Let me talk to her alone, y'all," Sunkist requested of Martinez and Koontz. They left, closing the door behind them.

Over the next week Fire and Sunkist talked, laughed, and planned their future. Fire even let Martinez sit and listen to them conversate, including her in their plans. Finally, the day came for Fire to be released.

Sunkist, Martinez, and Koontz went to pick her up from the hospital. Sunkist pulled into the parking lot and there was nowhere to park. The hospital was packed. He chose to drive up to the front of the hospital by the double doors. He parked and they went inside. Fire was ready to go. She was sitting in her wheelchair waiting on Sunkist. Martinez grabbed her bags for her. Sunkist bent down and kissed her. He got behind her and pushed her to the exit door.

As they got closer to the exit door there were hundreds of people standing outside the hospital. Sunkist pushed Fire through the exit door. Once they were outside the crowd erupted.

"We love you, Fire! Welcome home!" The city showed their love for a real gangsta. Out of the crowd came B.J. Pimp, Mike, Crimz, Boo, Mia, Deadly, and Souljah. Lil Don, Smooth, BK Red, Lil Weezy, Father, Sandman, Sumo, Tiny Harlem, and Tiny Diamond circled around Fire to show their love and respect. Sunkist looked at Martinez and Koontz knowing they are the ones that freed the rest of the family.

Today was a great day in the city of Fayetteville.

About the Author

Selo-Sunkist is from the streets of Fayetteville North Carolina. He is the CEO of Zionna fashion boutique and is involved in his community as an activist. He is also a motivational speaker and poet. He is on the front line helping pave the way for the less fortunate. Remember knowledge means nothing without knowing how to apply it.